P9-ARK-990

FRANCINE PROSE

Bullyville

HARPER TEEN
An Imprint of HarperCollinsPublishers

LIBRARY
FRANKLIN PIERCE UNIVERSITY
RINDGE, NH 03461

HarperTeen is an imprint of HarperCollins Publishers.

Bullyville

Copyright © 2007 by Francine Prose
All rights reserved.

Printed in the United States of America.

No part of this book may be used or reproduced in
any manner whatsoever without written permission except in the
case of brief quotations embodied in critical articles and reviews.
For information address HarperCollins Children's Books,
a division of HarperCollins Publishers,
1350 Avenue of the Americas,
New York, NY 10019.
www.harperteen.com

Library of Congress Cataloging-in-Publication Data

Prose, Francine.

Bullyville / Francine Prose. — 1st ed.

p. cm.

Summary: After the death of his estranged father in the World Trade Center on
9/11, thirteen-year-old Bart, still struggling with his feelings of guilt, sorrow and
loss, wins a scholarship to the local preparatory school and there encounters a
vicious bully whose cruelty compounds the aftermath of the tragedy.

ISBN 978-0-06-057497-0 (trade bdg.) — ISBN 978-0-06-057498-7 (lib. bdg.)

[1. Death—Fiction. 2. Grief—Fiction. 3. Bullies—Fiction. 4. Preparatory
schools—Fiction. 5. Schools—Fiction. 6. September 11 Terrorist Attacks,
2001—Fiction. 7. New Jersey—Fiction.] I. Title.

PZ7.P94347Bul 2007   2007006996

[Fic]—dc22   CIP

AC

Typography by Larissa Lawrynenko
1 2 3 4 5 6 7 8 9 10
❖
First Edition

For Bruno and Leon
and Yesenia — the
hope of the future

Bullyville

CHAPTER ONE

THE SCHOOL I WENT TO, that worst year of my life, was officially known as Baileywell Preparatory Academy. But everyone called it Bullywell Prep. Or Bullyville Prep. Or sometimes, Bully*really*well Prep. Because that was what it prepared you for. You learned to bully or be bullied, and to do it really well.

Perched high on a hill above our town so you could see it for miles, the school looked like a scaled-down, cheesy medieval castle. The walls were gray stones, large and rough as boulders. Once, in English class, a kid whom everyone

1

called Ex (as in, Can we do this *extra* thing for *extra* credit?) read a poem he'd written (for extra credit) about an ancient race of giants rolling stones up Bailey Mountain to build Baileywell Prep so that famous knights in armor could go there.

> *O Monster Masons!*
> *How we honor your dream*
>
> *That we Baileywellers would be in*
> *these seats today*
> *Like Lancelot and Aragorn*
> *Enjoying the fruits of your giant*
> *labors.*

The poem went on for about an hour. Or so it seemed, just as it seemed to me the giants must have been seriously retarded to imagine that King Arthur or the Lord of the Rings would want to attend a freezing, bully-ridden, all-boys boarding school on the highest point in Hillbrook, New Jersey. On clear days you could spot the school's tower barely peeping out from under the toxic cloud that hung constantly over our high-priced (if you didn't count our block) and rich (if you didn't count our family) but severely polluted suburb. The kids at Bullywell, most of whom came from somewhere else, called the town Hellbrook. The kids I'd grown up with called it Hellbrook, too, but that was our privilege, we'd earned it. It was our town, we'd lived there all our lives.

Among the things I never understood about Baileywell was why everything and everyone had to have a nickname. In all the time I was there, I never learned the real names of kids I knew only as Pork or Dog or Buff. The gym was "the sweat lodge," the dining hall—the *refectory*—was "the slop shop." Our headmaster, Dr. Bratton, was never called anything but Dr. Bratwurst. In fact, he did look a little like a sausage that had figured out how to walk around on remarkably tiny feet and wear glasses and one of those unstylish college-professor tweed jackets with leather patches on the elbows.

The school's main building, Bracknell Hall, was known as Break-knuckles Hall. It had a pointed roof and notched turrets. Most likely they were just meant to be decorative—unless some crazed architect actually imagined that a crack team of archers or sharpshooters might someday need to defend the school from an invading army. But who would want to capture it? No one even wanted to *go* there. A tower rose from the highest point on the roof, but no one ever climbed it. The entrance to the tower had been permanently bricked shut, supposedly for safety and insurance purposes.

But there was another story, which Bullywell students and the rest of the town did, and didn't, believe. People said that some long-ago bullies, pioneers of the school's great tradition, had chased their victim into the tower and sealed it off and he'd died there, and the school had hushed it up. On windy nights, people said, you could still hear the dead kid screaming for his mom and dad.

People told lots of stories about Bullywell

Prep. They said a gang of bullies had drowned one kid in a pot of split pea soup, and at lunch the next day his eyeballs bubbled up to the surface of the music teacher's bowl. They said that, in the dead of night, ambulances pulled up to the back gate and picked up kids who'd been bullied until they were hopelessly insane, and carted them off to mental asylums from which they never returned. They said that every year, at the Bullywell graduation, there was always one kid whose brain had been so destroyed he couldn't even remember how to say thank you when they handed him his diploma.

I'd heard all those stories—and scarier ones—before I started at Bullywell. But what happened to me there seemed even worse, I guess because it happened to me.

Through seventh grade, I'd gone, like most of the kids in my town, to Hillbrook Middle School. And before that, we'd all gone to Hillbrook Elementary. School was school, no one thought about it all that much. It was just a place we went, something we did every day.

In class, me and my friends had long ago figured out how to stay in constant communication and still keep quiet enough to not wind up in the principal's office. We listened—or pretended to listen—to our teachers. We did exactly as much homework as we had to, and not one minute, not one second, more. Already my mom had started saying I should begin thinking ahead, to college, but that was *way* much farther ahead than I could imagine.

As far as I was concerned, school was where I got to hang out with my friends, most of whom I'd known since the first grade. Lunch and gym were the best parts of the day, though none of us—me, Mike Bannerjee, Tim Reilly, Josh Levine, and Ted Nakamura—were all that good in gym. We didn't care about playing on the teams, but nobody gave us a hard time. The other kids seemed to like us okay. We were flying miles under the radar, and that was where we liked it. We laughed a lot, we had fun.

Looking back, I can see how safe and sheltered and naive we were. None of us realized how we should have been thanking our lucky stars that we were at Hillbrook rather than Baileywell.

At Hillbrook Middle School, even the teachers made jokes about Bullywell. When a kid acted up in class, a teacher might say something like, "Young man, maybe the best thing for you would be a semester at Baileywell." Then everyone would giggle nervously, as if the teacher had said that the best thing for the kid would be to smear him all over with honey and tie him down on an anthill swarming with stinging red ants.

Even then, I half suspected that the reason people talked so much about the school was probably that there was nothing else to talk about. Nothing ever happened in our town. No murders, no break-ins, not even a one-joint drug bust. There were two town cops, who, as far as I could tell, spent all their time giving out parking tickets on Main Street and rushing to the scene of an occasional fender bender. It was exciting to imagine that a chamber of horrors existed in plain sight on a hill above our town, and that cruel rich parents spent small fortunes to send their abused, unhappy children there.

There's a saying I heard once: Nothing happens. Nothing happens. Then everything happens. And that year I learned that, like so many sayings, it was not only true, but true in a way that no one could possibly have predicted. Not even in their worst nightmares.

For a long time, nothing happened. And then the Big Everything that happened was so terrible that we completely stopped making up stories about what went on at Bullywell. It was as if we could no longer imagine a world in which we would even *want* to spread terrifying rumors about a school. Because, as it turned out, real life was so much better at dreaming up horrors, real life had been dreaming up the *major* nightmare, all along.

Among the unwanted side effects of the Big Everything that happened was that I found myself transformed. My life, as I'd known it, was over. As if by magic, I was changed from an ordinary kid into a character in a fairy tale, into plucky, stupid little Jack scrambling up the beanstalk to find himself in a castle surrounded by evil giants masquerading as happy, healthy, well-adjusted Baileywell Bullies.

I started eighth grade at Hillbrook Middle School, the same as always, and, as always, the first days of school seemed to shine with a bright, hopeful light. The weather was sunny, and the outlines of everything looked slightly sharper and clearer, the way they do when summer is turning that corner into fall. Everyone had brand-new clothes and book bags, notebooks full of empty pages that gave off that clean-paper smell. And all of us (or anyway, me) were still promising ourselves that this year we'd try harder, like our moms (or anyway, mine) wanted us to. This year we'd actually get good grades instead of just getting by.

As always, there were a few awkward moments when my friends and I talked about what we'd done on vacation, and I remembered that their families were richer than mine. Not *that much* richer, but rich enough so they'd done cooler things over the summer. Ted and Mike had gone to fancy sleepaway camps, Josh and Tim had taken long trips with their parents. Me, I'd spent July and August swimming in my gran's above-ground pool, mowing the lawn for my various aunts, and occasionally babysitting my youngest cousins. But it only took a little while before I forgot all that, and I remembered how hilarious my friends could be, and how much fun it was when we got together.

And then one morning, a week or so after the beginning of eighth grade, I woke up and watched the globe on my bookshelf spin in swimmy circles without anyone touching it or being anywhere near it. I was freezing. I couldn't stop shivering. I called my mother into my room and asked her if she saw the globe spinning, too.

She put her cool hand on my forehead and said, "Dear God, what do we do now?"

Like any normal kid, I loved staying home from school sick. A little achiness and some shaking chills were nothing compared to the unlimited TV, all the juice you could drink, plenty of sympathetic or even worried looks from Mom, the occasional cold washcloth on your forehead. What could be better! But getting sick during the first week of school made it a little less perfect. I hadn't had time to get tired of school yet. I felt as if something important or even fun might be happening somewhere without me, and that I was missing it, and that I might never catch up or be allowed to join the party.

My mother liked my being sick even less than I did. She worked all day in the city, and I no longer had a regular babysitter she could call in emergencies. For the last year or so, I'd been allowed to stay home alone between the time I got home from school and when Mom got back from work. But *sick* changed the ground rules completely. My mother was no more capable of leaving me home alone sick than she was of levitating off the ground and flying me on her back, like an angel, all the way to her office in downtown Manhattan.

Perhaps this is the moment to say that, in case you haven't already figured it out, my dad no longer lived with us. He hadn't been around much for about six months. He had gone to live with a woman named Caroline, who was younger and who was supposed to be pretty. And as if that weren't *vile enough*, as my mom kept saying, Caroline worked in the same office as my mother and father. And she hadn't even had the decency to quit after she and my dad fell in love. *"Love!"* my mom would say, screwing up her face as if she'd bitten into a lemon. So there they were, in my mom's face, Monday to Friday, nine to five.

I didn't watch *that* much TV, but I'd seen enough talk shows and soap operas and made-for-TV films to know that a middle-aged married guy ditching his wife for a newer, hotter model was pretty standard operating procedure for middle-aged married guys. Or, as my mom put it, our whole situation was a "banal, humiliating cliché."

And there was one more odd detail, which was that my mom and I somehow hadn't gotten around to making a public announcement that my dad wasn't living with us anymore. Mom and I never exactly *planned* not to tell anyone. But the first time I heard Gran ask how Dad was and I heard Mom say that he was fine but just really busy, I knew that his leaving was going to be our weird little secret.

At first I was almost annoyed that Mom didn't complain more, that she didn't announce to the whole world what a creep Dad was and what he'd done to us. But after a while I decided it was fine with me, not having to tell my friends. I wasn't in a rush to broadcast the bad news.

Even though I knew plenty of kids with broken families and stepsiblings and the whole Brady Bunch situation, as far as I could see, divorce earned you an instant heavy dose of the wrong kind of attention. People felt sorry for you, and when it was time to arrange parent-teacher conferences, the teachers called you aside and got all gooey-eyed and asked, in a whisper, which of your parents was planning to show up. That wasn't how I wanted to end seventh grade or begin the eighth.

The main thing was, I don't think Mom was ready to tell *her* mom and her sisters, all of whom were supposedly happily married. So whenever Gran and my aunts came over, we made some excuse. Dad was working late, he was away on business, the boss had invited him to play golf and he couldn't refuse. If anyone noticed, or thought it was strange, no one seemed to want to talk about it, either. No one ever pointed out that Dad didn't even *play* golf and he'd never gone away on business. All of which made me realize that he'd been missing in action for a long time before he'd actually bailed and moved in with Caroline.

It's not as if Mom and I were the kind of lunatics who set a place at the dinner table for Dad every night and pretended he was coming home. We knew what the story was. My mom and dad had called a sort of family conference so they could tell me together that they were splitting up, and that they both still loved me and that it wasn't my fault. The usual routine that divorcing parents feel they have to go through. For the kids' sake. Everybody cried, even Dad. Only later, after Dad had moved out and taken most of his stuff, did Mom decide to tell me the Caroline part.

I knew it had to be tough for her, still working with the two of them in the same office. But when she came home from work, she left it at the office. We just didn't talk about Dad. It was if he didn't exist. We knew we were both really sad about his being gone. We just didn't need to say it. It was almost as if saying it would have made us feel even more abandoned and pathetic.

Most weekends, Dad called on the phone to speak to me. He and I had the sort of conversation ("What's new?" "Nothing." "How's school?" "Fine.") that would have been a totally normal parent-kid conversation if he'd still been part of the family. But now that he was gone, it seemed like some kind of big drama in which I was *refusing* to talk. And when Dad asked if we could hang out together—and, to tell the truth, he'd been asking that less and less often—Mom told him that they would work all that out in the divorce settlement, but that she and I were both feeling too fragile now. I didn't like being called fragile, but I let it go, for Mom's sake.

After that, Dad started calling me on my cell phone and sending me text messages telling me he still loved me, but I never answered them, and when I recognized his number, I didn't pick up. Every so often—and, of course, I wouldn't have told anyone this—I called Dad at work. I had a whole speech prepared in my mind, a speech in which I told him exactly what he'd done to us and I asked him how he could have done it. But I always got his voice mail, and I never left a message.

Unfortunately, all this meant that we couldn't call Dad when Mom needed someone to stay home with me that September day when I was sick. She phoned Gran and Aunt Anita and then the other aunts—Aunt Grace and Aunt Barbara and Aunt Faye—in order of how much she liked them. But they'd all left for work. She called Ivy, the totally hot high school girl who used to babysit me. But it turned out that Ivy had left for her freshman year of college.

Mom hung up the phone and said, "How could Ivy be grown up? How could she be in college already?" And it was that, as much as anything else, that convinced Mom to call in to work and pretend that *she* was sick, so she could stay home with me.

When the phone rang, almost immediately, we thought it might be Gran or one of the aunts calling back. Mom answered. Then the phone rang again.

And after that it didn't stop ringing for days.

CHAPTER TWO

ALL THE NEWSPAPERS said the same thing—
word for word, more or less, with only
slight variations. A couple of them spelled my
name wrong, and, as if the truth wasn't dramatic
enough, one paper—out in Colorado, I think—
said I'd been home sick with pneumonia. At first I
wondered how they'd found out about me. Did a
neighbor tell them, or maybe someone from
school? And then I stopped wondering because,
by then, the papers were telling each other.

The headline and the story that followed
always went something like this:

SON'S ILLNESS SPARES TWIN TOWERS MOM

NOTHING was lucky about last Tuesday, but one Hillbrook, New Jersey, family has at least something to be thankful for. Bart Rangely's mom, Corinne, was due to go to work on the ninety-fifth floor of the North Tower of the World Trade Center. But because Bart, 13, a Hillbrook Middle School eighth grader, was running a high fever, his mother decided to stay home from work.

Bart's dad, Jim, wasn't so lucky. He also worked on the ninety-fifth floor, where he and Corinne had met at their jobs and had remained for more than fifteen years in the same office.

That morning he went in to work and is still among the missing. A somber mood hangs over the Rangely home as they wait for news of their loved one.

But at least, thanks to Bart's sudden illness, total disaster was averted.

Total disaster was averted. That's what my relatives seemed to feel, when, one by one, they called up. Gran and the aunts dialed our house first, on blind instinct, even though they were perfectly aware that Mom (and Dad, for all they knew, even though they hadn't seen much of him, or even asked about him, for quite a while) would have left for work earlier. So Mom and Dad, unless some miracle had happened—if, for example, they had missed their trains or the trains were running late—would already have been in the buildings that were now burning.

When Mom told them that she hadn't found anyone to stay with me and she'd stayed home, I could practically hear them thinking that it *had* been a miracle, my saving her life with my cold or flu or whatever it was. Then I'd hear Mom telling Gran and the aunts that, no, she hadn't heard from Dad—which was true. Then she'd tell them not to cry, that he'd probably got out in time, that everything was probably all right. And then they would all start to cry, because nothing was all right, and wouldn't be, ever again.

Was it a miracle? I didn't know. I didn't think so. It seemed more like something halfway between a lucky break and a coincidence. Every time I thought about my mother being in that building, I felt as if I was about to throw up.

Of course, we didn't know where Dad was. At first there was only confusion, and phone calls from cops, and then a call from someone in the firm who said that he was sorry to tell us, but Dad had probably been inside the tower.

And then, amazingly, Caroline called to say she was almost a hundred percent sure he'd been in the office. He'd left the apartment ahead of her. They'd stayed up late the night before and she'd wanted to sleep in.

"You stayed up late? You wanted to sleep in?" My mother kept saying that over and over, her voice getting louder and shriller each time until she finally made herself thank Caroline for calling, and hung up. Neither of us said what we were both thinking: that we couldn't help wishing it

had been Caroline who'd been killed instead of Dad.

After Mom got off the phone with Caroline, neither of us knew what to say. We couldn't speak. Mom walked over to my bed with her arms already outstretched to hug me. And the strange thing was that before I even felt sad or sorry for myself and Mom, I felt sort of . . . embarrassed by the whole thing. It was bad enough that Dad might be dead—that he probably *was* dead. But it was worse to still feel my anger at him mixed in with the shock and the sorrow. I started cursing out Caroline, but Mom said, "We should thank her for wanting us to know and for having the courage to tell us."

"Right," I said. "Thanks a million."

Mom put her hand on my forehead.

"You're burning up," she said. And though it was totally bizarre and inappropriate, I thought: Like Dad.

Like before, we didn't talk about Dad. But now, obviously, everything was different. And we almost didn't have to mention him, because we had this secret that partway protected us from our own grief, and from the river of grief that was flowing all around us, and everywhere, in those days.

In the parking lot of the railroad station in our town were four cars that no one drove home that night. Plus there had been some carpooling. So I guess that Hillbrook should have been declared a national disaster area. Which it basically was.

Reporters were swarming all over our town, and most of them wound up at our house when they wanted a feel-good moment to wrap up their terrible day. My dad was dead—most likely dead—but the fact that I still had a mom counted as a feel-good moment.

There was black bunting everywhere, black and purple and American flags. It looked as if they were giving the entire town a military funeral. At 10:28 each morning, the mall flickered its lights. No one knew who started that, just as no one noticed when the freaky new custom ended.

And in the middle of it all, I was the Miracle

Boy, the lucky orphan. The kid who lost his dad but saved his mother's life. I had everything, grief and hope, tragedy and consolation, wrapped up in one neat package. Me. I felt like a total liar, except that I wasn't lying about the most important thing, which was that my father had been killed and I would never get over it. Ever. It was hard enough trying to get my mind around what had happened to *me*—to us—without the added strangeness of my dad's death being part of some major, public, historic event that had happened to thousands of other families, and to the city, the country, the world.

The flu or whatever it was lasted three more days, then disappeared as quickly as it had come. Still, I could make myself sick all over again by letting myself think about what a tiny window—a few degrees of fever, *my* fever—had made a difference between having a mom and not having a mom. So I tried not to think about it, and Mom and I didn't talk about *that*, either, though we probably should have.

We didn't have time! The phone was always ringing, someone was always at the door, someone was always apologizing for intruding at such a sad and private moment. Someone was always bringing a casserole or asking for an interview. The kids in my school took up a collection and bought me three new PlayStation games that my friend Mike Bannerjee dropped off while his dad waited outside in their Volvo with the engine running.

It was strange, seeing Mike like that. He'd been the funniest of all my friends. But no one was joking around now, and we didn't know what to say. He kept looking over his shoulder, as if he couldn't wait to hop back in his dad's car and drive away. I thought: At least he still has a dad! I didn't like how that made me feel, and suddenly I realized that going back to school would be hard and painful and weirdly . . . embarrassing.

I wasn't sure I could do it. Maybe I'd never have to go back. Maybe I could talk Mom into homeschooling. But I knew that wasn't an option. With Dad no longer sending us money, she *had* to go back to work as soon as there was somewhere for her to go back to. And I didn't want to make her feel worse by letting her know how much I dreaded returning to Hillbrook.

Meanwhile, we could hardly go out, because someone had to be home to accept all the presents. First came the flowers, the chocolate, the cheer-up teddy bears that I couldn't even let myself hate because I knew the people who sent them had meant so well. But did they really think a stuffed bear would help make up for not having a dad?

Then the big presents started arriving. The UPS man, Carmine Genovese, became our new best friend, as he showed up, looking properly stricken, to deliver the hams, the breads, the baskets of soap, the year's supply of laundry detergent. The gift box of books that ranged from picture books to YA novels, as if the giver didn't quite know how old I was or what my reading level might be. It didn't matter, I couldn't read any of them, I couldn't concentrate for that long.

Someone sent us a certificate for a free water-purity test. Some other kind person thought our loss might make us aware of our need for a free termite inspection. But we didn't have termites—or anyway, this wasn't the moment when we wanted to find out that we did.

Mom handed most of the gifts over to Gran and my aunts and said to keep them, or to give them to someone who needed them. The worst part was that Mom thought she had to thank everyone who sent us a note or a present, and it took up a lot of time. Or maybe that was the best part: It took up a lot of time. Mom wrote lots of notes, and when we ran into people on Main Street, we thanked them in person. We thanked the butcher, the girl in the soap store, the guy who owned the bookshop. Everyone said they were sorry for our loss, and we'd all bow our heads and look tragic. And then almost everyone found some way to say how amazing it was that I'd been sick, how lucky for my mom, and then everyone got happy again. Or halfway happy.

Before, our neighbors had been friendly, but now they couldn't do enough for us. Suddenly Mom and I were like the mayors of the town. And I was the Miracle Boy. I was half afraid that, if I didn't watch out, people might start praying to me.

Some mornings, I had to go out and clean up the flowers and candles and notes that people had left at the end of our driveway. They even brought their kids' drawings of how they imagined Mom and me: two stick figures holding hands with the towers blazing behind us. We became local celebrities. Everyone knew who we were. And when people saw us in the street, or in a shop, sometimes even in the mall, I could see them trying to arrange their faces into what they thought was the correct way to express their sympathy. Usually it was a sheepish smile, as if they were looking at a newborn baby or an extremely cute puppy.

Every so often distant relatives would send us a newspaper clipping from their hometown paper in which we were described as the family whose kid had had that lucky case of flu. But I didn't feel lucky, not even a tiny bit lucky. My father was dead. How could any sane person have called that lucky?

At first when Dad had left us, I'd been so mad, I'd tried not to think about him, the way Mom and I tried not to talk about him. Then I let myself miss him a little, and until he actually got killed, I'd pretty much gotten used to missing him. It was something you could get used to, like everything else.

But now I was shocked by how different this was. Because in the back of my mind I'd always secretly believed that he'd realize—he'd *have* to realize—that Caroline was a mindless twit, as Mom called her. And he'd get sick of how young and pretty and stupid she was. Then he'd come back, and Mom would forgive him, and we'd all be together again, with Dad and Mom bickering like before, like any normal parents.

But now this new . . . I didn't know what to call it. Now this new *development* had totally ruined any chance of *that* ever happening. That dream was over. Definitely. And I was really really sad. I kept remembering little details, tiny things about Dad—the way his glasses used to slip down his nose; the clumsy, flat-footed run he had when we played catch; the way he'd pick me up and swing me around when he came home from work until I got so big that he'd groan and complain that his back hurt. When I let myself think about that, I'd go in my room and cry. To tell the truth, it didn't help all that much to imagine how much worse things could have been if I hadn't run a fever that morning.

After a week, I went back to school, but it was like one of those bad dreams in which everyone you know is there but they all seem to be in the wrong place, and nothing that they do or say makes any sense. Everything was a blur, until some kid's face would come into focus just long enough for him to tell me how sorry he was. The girls were superkind to me, and some of them even cried when they saw me, but it just made me feel weak, like some pitiful freak loser. None of my friends, or the kids I knew from before, treated me like the same person, and the new teachers hadn't known me long enough to know *what* kind of person I was. My old teachers were nice enough, really nice. Too bad I wasn't in their classes.

I made it through two days. Then I asked Mom if I could stay home from school for a while longer. I said I still wasn't feeling that great. Though she looked concerned, she said, "Sure, honey, let's let a little time pass, and then we'll see what's what."

Being home was like staying home sick, except with no TV. Because every time I turned the television on, we had to watch the towers burning. And neither Mom nor I could stand to see that.

My mother didn't go back to the office. There was no office for her to go to. She seemed to spend all her time filling out forms and talking to lawyers. Her mom and sisters kept urging her—and me—to join a support group so we could get together with the other 9/11 families. But we didn't want to.

It would have been hard to find the right group—the group made up of kids and parents whose moms or dads (or husbands or wives) had abandoned the family six months before that September.

Later it occurred to me that, in any group we joined, there might have been people in our situation, or at least something like it. Why not? With so many people, so many different lives, things like that *had* to happen. But by the time that occurred to me, it was already too late. We'd gotten used to toughing it out, to going it alone.

Every so often, I'd read the "Portraits of Grief," those mini-obituaries of people killed on 9/11, in *The New York Times*. Mostly I looked for the ones in which you could tell that the person wasn't all that popular or cool. This one had overcome what his survivors called "some problems"; that one had obviously been hard to work with, or difficult to live with. Most of the victims sounded as if they'd been lovable and saintly, but the screwed-up ones, the creepy ones—those were the stories that made me feel better. For about a minute.

After the *Times* reporter assigned to Dad's "Portrait of Grief" finally called us, the piece that appeared was the same old, same old about my saving my mom by being sick that day and how it would have made my dad feel better to know that I wasn't all alone in the world, that Mom had survived to take care of me. But how much better could he feel, considering that he was dead?

Already they'd started busting people for lying about losing family members, either so everyone would feel sorry for them or so they could collect the compensation money that we were supposedly going to get. Every time I read a story like that, I wondered if Mom and I were guilty of something sort of like that. I told myself we weren't. My real dad had really been killed. I hadn't made it up. The fact that he wasn't living with us hardly counted, compared to how horribly he'd died, and the fact that he was gone forever.

My mom had started tucking me in again at night, like she used to when I was little. And once, when I was half asleep, I heard myself sort of mumbling, asking Mom if she thought we should tell someone . . .

I didn't have to finish my sentence. She knew what I meant.

She said, "We don't *have* to do anything. Except get through this and take care of each other. That's all. That's our job now."

It crossed my mind that now I might *never* have to tell anyone that my dad had left us before he got killed. I wondered about when I grew up and got married. Would I have to tell my wife and kids? Or would I take it with me to my grave like some terrible deep dark secret?

Time passed in a strange way, sometimes fast, sometimes slow. One day I woke up and it was October. That was the day my mother got a letter from the headmaster of Baileywell Preparatory Academy.

Sometimes, when the mail was piled so high that it threatened to topple off the dining room

night when Dad was driving.

It wasn't helpful to think about Dad at that particular moment. I watched Dr. Bratton bounce up our front walk as if he were coming to sell us life insurance, or convert us to some perverted new religion. To this day, I don't know why he came to see us instead of summoning us to his office in the heart of the heart of the castle. Maybe he wanted to observe us in our natural surroundings, maybe he wanted to see for himself the house where the half miracle, half tragedy had occurred, or maybe (and he would have been right about that, at least) he thought that Mom and I were too (as Mom said) *fragile*. We might never have accepted an invitation to come see him in his office. The strain and the effort would have been too much.

Because by that point, Mom was not in her most reliable get-out-of-bed-bright-and-early-every-morning mode. In fact, we'd both slipped into a kind of dream state. We didn't go out much, we mostly stayed home with the curtains closed and lay on my mom's king-sized bed, the bed that used to be Mom and Dad's. By then we'd learned to navigate our way around the disaster newsreel footage and avoid the burning towers and the choking survivors stumbling through clouds of dust. We spent a lot of time watching *Law & Order* reruns.

Everyone understood. When Gran and my aunts drove over to bring casseroles and clean the house and do our laundry, they tiptoed around and whispered as if the slightest disturbance would make us shatter into a million tiny pieces. And they were right. It would have.

It had all come down on Mom at once: Dad's death, their separation, her own near miss. In fact, I thought that Dad's dying that way just wiped out the whole part about the separation and brought Mom back to the place where she and Dad were a more or less happy couple with a kid, a house in the suburbs, and the two jobs in the city. That was what she missed, and now that she'd forgotten the detail about having to see Dad and Caroline every day, she also missed going to work. Every once in a while, she got calls from relatives of other people from her office; most of her coworkers were dead. The relatives asked how she was doing, and passed along the latest rumors about compensation payments and how the company might move somewhere else and start all over again. Mom didn't seem to care about that, or about anything much.

One day, someone called from the city coroner's office asking her if she could bring in Dad's toothbrush so they could match his DNA to whatever they found at the site. That drove Mom straight back to bed. She hadn't felt like telling them that he'd taken his toothbrush with him when he moved in with Caroline.

Once, Mom said she was glad that Dad's parents were dead. They'd both been killed in a car wreck not long before I was born. She'd liked them, they were sweet and kind, and it was fortunate they hadn't lived to see this. I didn't think it was so fortunate. I wished I had more grandparents. I wished

I had all the family it was possible to have.

Every so often, Mom would haul herself into the living room and sit straight across from me and stare into my eyes and say, "I know this is hard for you, baby. I want you to be able to talk about it to me. You need to talk about it. We're going through this together."

But what was I supposed to say? I missed Dad, and the whole Twin Towers thing made me feel terrified and sick. If I said that, how was it going to help Mom? So I didn't talk about it, I got used to not talking about it, and after a while I sort of *liked* not talking about it. It made me feel in control, grown-up. Manly. I thought that my keeping my mouth shut was what Dad would have wanted.

I kept hoping Mom would get better, but she seemed to be getting worse. She almost never wanted to leave the house. She sent me out to the convenience store—the nearest one I could walk to—for small grocery items. The supermarket delivered, and we ordered a lot of takeout. Chinese, Indian, Mexican—we didn't eat much, anyway. I Googled her behavior—her symptoms—on the internet. That was how I found out that Mom might be suffering from PTSD, post-traumatic stress disorder. I don't think it helped her to know that she'd just been a few degrees (my fever!) away from getting killed, herself.

She stopped driving, and in the back of my mind I was beginning to worry that she was becoming a serious problem I was going to have to deal with. Should I tell Gran or my aunts? Mom got dressed for their visits, which meant that she hadn't totally run off the rails. And even if she hadn't gotten dressed, even if she'd greeted them in her nightgown, in bed, they would have accepted that, too.

And so when it turned out that Dr. Bratton was coming to see us, and it seemed like the first thing that had gotten Mom excited, or even interested, in weeks, I felt I had to get with the program. Fine, let the dude come visit. Let him get a good look at Mom in her bathrobe, with her hair unwashed. Let him see what basket cases we were.

Let him satisfy his sick curiosity about our semi-tragedy. And then let him regret the fact that, in his letter, he'd mentioned the possibility of my going to Baileywell Preparatory Academy on a full scholarship, a new and specially earmarked endowment from an anonymous donor.

In five minutes he'd be telling himself that he hadn't really made an offer, hadn't promised or committed himself. It had only been a *possibility* that was, after all, impossible. He could tell the anonymous donor that I was academically unqualified, that it wouldn't be good for me *or* the school to admit me at this point. Maybe they could keep looking until they found some worthy, high-achieving kid whose dad had been an undocumented restaurant worker at Windows on the World.

On the morning of Dr. Bratton's visit, Mom practically skipped downstairs in pressed jeans and a bright red sweater. Her hair and face were shining. She looked like a mother in a TV commercial, waking up early to prepare her family big bowls of the hottest, steamingest, healthiest breakfast cereal.

"Dr. Bratton! Come in," my mother said. "Would you like some coffee?"

I suppose I shouldn't have been surprised. But I *was* surprised, and scared. And the part that scared me most was this: Ever since my dad got killed, Mom would say, "I know people talk about good things coming out of bad things. But I wish someone could show me *one* good thing that's coming out of this. I don't count bombing Afghanistan, or some yuppie couple meeting as they fled up Fifth Avenue in the rain of ashes, or the wake-up call about terrorism, or the flag stuff, or the rest of that. And I don't count my surviving. I mean, this thing didn't *make* me live, it almost killed me. It *would* have killed me if you hadn't been sick. And not being killed doesn't count as something good coming out of something bad."

I hated it when she talked like that. Because I didn't feel I could tell her what I really thought:

45

Nothing good was going to come out of this. Sometimes bad things happen, and they're just bad. End of story. No compensation. No points earned for suffering. But no one wants to listen to philosophy from a thirteen-year-old, not even the thirteen-year-old's mother.

It wasn't until I watched Mom working to make a good impression on bouncy Dr. Bratton that I realized that my being offered a full scholarship to the fanciest, snootiest, most expensive school in northern New Jersey could have been seen by someone—not by me!—as something good coming out of something bad. In fact, my going to Baileywell was what Mom had always secretly—well, not secretly at all—wanted. To me, it was more as if something bad was leading to something even worse. I would explain that to my mom later, as soon as Dr. Bratton left. And it would have been fine with me if he'd left right away.

When had Mom made coffee? Dr. Bratton took his with tons of milk and sugar. We settled in the couch, from which the plastic cups and Chinese-food containers and pizza boxes must have been removed by elves in the middle of the night.

Dr. Bratton sipped his coffee. All his gestures had a kind of delicate, chirpy grace that I couldn't quite put together with the headmaster of a school for manly bullies and future masters of the universe. Frankly, he reminded me a little of my aunt Grace, who had married a big mafioso and somehow managed to turn into a British person.

"I'm so sorry for your loss," Dr. Bratton said, and we all did that sheepish nod.

"It's been hard," said Mom in a way that made her seem even prettier than normal.

"I can imagine," said Dr. Bratton. "I mean, I *can't* imagine."

"You can't, actually," said Mom. A silence fell, and we stared at one another. The ball was in his court.

He tapped his fingertips together, as if he was afraid they might be sizzling hot and he was testing

47

them to make sure. Then he joined them into a peak, like a church roof, with its spire just under his nose, as if he was sniffing the steeple.

"Like everyone else in this country, in the *world*," he said, "the Baileywell community has been asking itself what can we possibly do. How can we help, how can we make a difference, how can we react to this terrible tragedy that has shaken us to the core? Of course, a number of our parents and faculty have been going to work as volunteers at Gro—"

He stopped short as he got to "Ground Zero." He'd remembered who we were.

"And then we read the inspiring, hopeful story about you and your son, having lost so much and having been saved, by sheer chance, really, from losing so much more. And what I want to tell you, Mrs. Rangely, is that it wasn't your tragedy so much as the whole scenario: a mother who chose her child's needs over those of her job, a mother who even now must continue to put her professional life on hold because her orphaned child needs her. And the simple eloquence and dignity with which you, Bart, have dealt with the reporters and with all the interviews that must have been so terribly painful."

"To tell you the truth, I was pretty numb," I said. "It was sort of like I'd gotten a big shot of Novocain. So the interviews weren't all *that* painful." In fact, I could hardly remember any of my conversations with the reporters. I was about to say that, but I stopped because Mom and Dr. Bratton were staring at me as if they couldn't quite figure out what I was doing there, or if I was speaking English.

After a pause, Dr. Bratton said, "I wish I could claim this was my idea. But to be perfectly truthful, the inspiration first occurred to one of our more creative parents, who also happens to be one of our most supportive and generous donors. He was reading the paper, and he saw the article about you two, and he immediately called me and said, 'This is the kind of student, the kind of moral fiber, the kind of wisdom and maturity we want in our Baileywell population.' Naturally I agreed right away."

Wisdom and maturity? What were they talking about? Two planes flew into a building. My dad died. I had the flu. My mom stayed home. What was so wise and mature about that?

"So," he went on, "we would like to offer Brad—"

"Bart," said my mom.

"Of course. Bart," said Dr. Bratton. "As I believe I mentioned in my letter, we would like to offer Bart a full scholarship to Baileywell, all expenses paid, even including transportation in the van we run for our day students."

"That's so generous of you," said Mom. "Everyone knows that Baileywell is such an amazing school!"

Dr. Bratton smiled shyly—and proudly. "This is not the moment, I know, to burden you with the statistics of how many of our graduates go on to Harvard, Yale, and Stanford, and other similarly elite institutions."

"Stanford's awfully far," said Mom.

"Columbia," said Dr. Bratton. "Harvard."

"How marvelous," said Mom

Great, I thought. Just what I want. An elite institution.

"What's more important even than college," Dr. Bratton continued, "are the lifelong friendships that Baileywell students form, relationships that are not only sustaining in every way, but are incredibly helpful as our graduates find their path through a world that gets scarier and more threatening every day. Sadly, it's not the same world we knew when you and I got out of college."

"You can say that again," said Mom.

Could she and Dr. Bratton really be the same age? He acted about a hundred years older.

"And what's *most* important"—Dr. Bratton seemed to be on automatic pilot, so that I wondered if this was a speech he gave all the time—"is the kind of young men we are graduating. Men who feel sympathy for the underdog. The little guy. Who can see things from the little guy's point of view. Our hope is that the Baileywell experience will produce the sort of compassionate, feeling, deeply human men who will lead us into a brighter and more caring future."

"Compassion. The future could *use* that," Mom said, and there was another loaded silence.

"Because we are essentially a boarding institution," Dr. Bratton said at last, "we have a rich afternoon program. A whole range of after-school activities, though of course it's not *after* for our boarding students. We have a wide variety of athletics to choose from. Theater. Art." He looked at me as if he was trying to tell if I'd be a rugby player or a theater or art type. "Of course, the day-student bus would bring Brad—"

"Bart," I said.

"The bus would bring Bart home probably around the same time you'd be returning from work, Mrs. Rangely."

Work? What work? Obviously Dr. Bratton knew nothing, nothing about us.

"That would be great," said Mom, as if there

were a job that she went to every day and would perform more efficiently knowing that I was getting soccer balls kicked in my face by the bullies up the hill.

I sent her an urgent mental telegraph: *Please, no. Forget about it. Let's pull the plug on this right now.* But for some reason my transmission just wasn't getting through.

"It would be great for me to know he was being so well taken care of until I got home from work," she went on. Had Mom taken a new job that I didn't know about? No, she'd entered a fantasy world in which she *had* a job, a world in which bad things led to at least *one* good thing: a free ride for her only son at the snobbiest school in the state.

By now I was practically waving my arms. *Don't do this, Mom! Don't you know that school's a snake pit of monsters waiting to jump out of the shadows and pounce on me the minute I walk in the door?* But how could I even begin to say that when Mom was talking about going back to work as if she already had, when my mother and Dr. Bratton were discussing *education*, talking about my future as if a bright, hopeful future existed?

When Dr. Bratton finally left, Mom said, "So what to do you think?"

I said, "I think the guy's about ten minutes away from being busted for downloading kiddie porn."

Mom stared at me for a moment. "That's *so* bad," she said. "You're awful!"

Then she starting laughing, she laughed out loud, and that was all that mattered. I decided to let the rest of it go. Mom was—for the moment—happy.

FOUR

WHEN I WAS LITTLE, I'd read a novel about a Nazi concentration camp where they made the prisoners, especially kids, pretend to be cheerful and healthy and having fun whenever the Red Cross inspectors came. I was probably too young for the book. I remember it gave me nightmares, which merged into an old nightmare that I'd had for as long as I could remember. In that dream, I was being kidnapped or killed. Mom and Dad were right there, but somehow they couldn't hear me, they couldn't save me, they couldn't help me in any way.

When I thought about going to Baileywell, all I could think about was that dream. I told myself it was just a dream, but I couldn't stop feeling that it was about to come true.

A few days before I was scheduled to start school, Dr. Bratton invited Mom and me to take a tour. I guess he wanted us to know what a valuable, precious prize we were getting, absolutely free of charge.

Mom dressed up as if she were going to work—or to a job interview. We drove up to the school on a winding road that snaked through a forest of red and orange maples. Even the trees seemed brighter and bigger and healthier than the trees down below. When we actually pulled up inside that insane fortress, the contrast between all the glorious brightness and the bleak, gray stone was so drastic and dramatic that all we could do was shrug and look at each other.

"My God," Mom said. "It looks like one of those fake medieval hotels by the side of Highway

One where people go to get married and spend their honeymoon drinking champagne in the Jacuzzi in the Dungeon Suite."

"If only," I said. "If only *that's* what went on here." Just at that moment, Dr. Bratton bounced out of the heavy cast-iron door, which clanged shut behind him. He skipped down the steps, trailed by a student.

My future tormentor. Tyro Bergen.

Later, though not much later, his monstrous qualities would emerge. Then he looked like what he was: a fiend in a horror movie. But when we first saw him, he seemed normal. Tall, thin, blond, and maybe just a little too handsome to pass for a regular kid. More like a movie star auditioning for the role of a prep school student.

"Tyro's one of our juniors," said Dr. Bratton. "Our seniors are so busy right now with their college applications, we generally don't ask them to be our Mentors and Big Brothers."

"Mentors and Big Brothers," said Mom. "How nice!"

"It's great," said Tyro, so tonelessly that the three of us turned and stared at him.

"Next year," my mom told Tyro, "you'll be applying to college. And then you're on your way."

Tyro didn't answer.

"You'll like it here," Tyro told me, in that same robotic voice.

Later, I couldn't believe that this Tyro was the same kid I got to know in ways that I never wanted to know anyone. None of the kids I met that day looked anything like they did later. And it wasn't just that strange thing that always happens—how someone looks totally different when you get to know that person better. I mean, I never again saw anyone remotely like the students I saw on that tour, those contented clones and science fiction pod-babies smiling like store-window dummies as they eagerly raised their hands and shouted out answers in every class we visited, as they ran themselves red in the face on the soccer field and tennis courts.

At every stop, Mom and I nodded and oohed

and aahed as if Dr. Bratton were a realtor and we were planning to buy the place instead of just go to school there. Which I wasn't. I still hadn't accepted the fact that I was doomed to go to Bullywell.

I was hoping for a miracle to save me from what seemed more and more unavoidable and dreadful, even as everything seemed to make my mom more and more hopeful and energetic. Which was strange, because I'd learned to stop hoping for a miracle. If there *were* miracles, my dad would have come walking in the door, maybe a little dusty and rattled, but alive and well and saying he'd ditched Caroline and wanted to come back home and live with us forever.

The point we were supposed to be getting, the point that Mom *was* getting, was that Baileywell was paradise. Teenage-boy paradise! By the time the tour ended, my mom and Dr. Bratton were practically embracing and weeping tears of joy on each other's shoulders. Without anyone consulting me or asking my opinion, it was decided that I would start school on October 15, just a few days away but long enough for us to locate the papers proving that I'd been vaccinated against rabies or whatever, and to shop for the gross navy blue blazers that made Baileywell students look like the boring businessmen-in-training that they were.

The moment had come to stop playing along and being cooperative and considerate. It was high time to quit pretending to be what Mom called "open to new ideas," to quit trying to make Mom feel more positive about life. The moment had come to stop imagining that something or someone was going to rescue me. It was time to save my own ass!

Starting on the drive home from Baileywell and continuing without mercy for the next few days, I begged my mom not to send me there. I tried every trick I knew. I argued and pleaded, I told her that Bullywell wouldn't expose me to the *real* world the way that Hillbrook Middle School would. I told her that everyone called it Bullywell, that it was full of bullies and snobs. Mom said *that* was the real world, I might as well get used to it now. I told her some of the stories: the dead kid in the tower, the eyeballs in the soup. I said they bullied kids to *death* there.

"Urban legends," Mom said. "Did you ever hear the one about the Doberman that bit off the burglar's finger? Or the human finger in the fast-food burger? Or the killer whose fingers got caught in the automatic car window? What's with all these stories about fingers, anyhow?"

Obviously Mom wasn't focusing. By then I was so desperate, I asked her if, considering how recently I'd lost my dad, she honestly thought I was ready to take on a possibly hostile new environment, to make a major change I didn't want to make.

I shouldn't have tried that one with Mom, I should have known it wouldn't work. Mom looked blankly in my general direction, and then her eyes left my face and drifted in the direction that, she must have imagined, led to Baileywell. It was as if she was *seeing* Baileywell, seeing the future that awaited us there: a new world, a castle where the drawbridge would be lowered, the gates opened, and where she and I would cross the moat and enter a place that would be safe from planes and bombs, defended and protected from anyone who might be planning to hurt us.

On the very next day after our tour of Bullywell Prep, Mom got a call informing her that her old company, the one where she'd worked with Dad, had found new headquarters—in New Jersey this time, much closer to our home. She was one of the people they were putting in charge of stitching together the scraps of what was left of their hearts and their minds and their business.

My mother went on a giant shopping spree, as if she had to buy a whole new wardrobe for the whole new person who was taking the whole new job. She tried on all her new outfits for me, and I told her how great she looked. Except for the fact that they still had their labels attached, the skirts and suits and jackets were almost identical to the ones she'd worn to her office in the North Tower, but I wasn't about to mention that.

Two days before I started at Baileywell, she went back to work. Even though she knew that she was supposed to be forgiving, even though she understood that our tragic experience was supposed to have made her a better person, the first thing she did was to fire Caroline. The second thing she did was to call and tell me.

"Way to go, Mom!" I said.

So all that seemed like another sign that there *was* a future for us, and that my future had bought me a first-class ticket on the express train to Bullywell. I even tried to act happy about it, by which I meant that on the first morning that the Baileywell day-student bus pulled up in front of our house to pick me up, I refrained from digging in my heels and hanging on to Mom's skirt and throwing a full-blown, kindergarten-style tantrum.

The driver was a hugely overweight guy whose folds of flesh hung down over the seat, so that the seat looked like a pedestal growing straight out of his butt. His thick arms surrounded the wheel, which he held between his surprisingly delicate fingers.

"Hi," I said, extending my hand. "I'm Bart Rangely."

The driver scowled at my hand, as if shaking it would constitute a dangerous breach of the rules of road safety, even though the bus was parked. Then he grunted and jerked his head toward the back of the bus, where my fellow day students waited.

My fellow day students! I remembered my dad quoting a comedian who used to say he wouldn't want to join any club that would admit him. Now, it seemed, I had been admitted to a club like that. Not only didn't I want to join it, but it was dangerous for me even to know it *existed*. The bus population looked like a casting call for the latest Hollywood nerd extravaganza or for one of those TV reality shows on which a superhot fashion model is asked to choose a husband from a selection of the ugliest guys on the planet.

It was hard to know if the admissions director had a secret preference for kids who looked like rabbits and chickens, or if they'd once looked normal and had been turned, by their experiences at Bullywell, into human versions of the most timid or stupid creatures in the food chain. That's what it must have been, because really, the day students weren't more wimpy or poor or stupid than the boarders. Their only crime was that they lived in the area, and their parents liked having them come home at night. But the boarders looked down on the day students, and little by little, I guess, the day students had begun to look like the losers everyone thought they were.

As I made my way to the back of the bus, they all looked up and then went back to staring silently and miserably out the window. It reminded me of prison vans I'd seen transporting handcuffed and chained passengers. I also thought of how, every once in a while, I'd made the mistake of looking through the back window of an ambulance and seen the face of some terrified relative they'd allowed to ride along with the patient.

"Hi, guys!" I said.

No one replied. No one smiled or nodded or turned as I walked past them and found an empty seat near the back of the bus.

I was careful not to make eye contact with anyone. I looked out the window. I was careful not to make eye contact with anyone's *reflection*.

The road that wound up to the castle—that is, the school—looked nothing like the one I'd taken just a few days before with Mom. That day had been sunny, but now the sky was the color of the stuffing of a ripped-apart old mattress that someone had left out in the weather. Between then and now, the wind must have blown all the bright autumn leaves off the trees, leaving bare branches that pointed at me like fingers promising some cruel punishment I must have done something to deserve. And as we traveled in the groaning bus, Bailey Mountain seemed higher and craggier than I remembered, and the climb took much longer than it had when Mom and I were in the car making nervous conversation.

We passed the main entrance and pulled up to a side door, as if the bus had come to deliver office supplies or cafeteria food instead of to be welcomed by the friendly, inclusive student community Dr. Bratton had described. Well, sure, the bus had come to deliver *us*, packages of something that no one actually seemed to want. And the packages didn't seem to want to be delivered.

As the day students trudged off the bus, they really did look like criminals, filing out of their transport to do some especially nasty roadwork detail. The bus emptied, but still I remained in my seat until the driver—who, I would later learn, everyone called Fat Freddie—yelled, "Last stop, pal. Everybody out. How much farther do you think we're going?"

I laughed as if that was the funniest thing anyone ever said. And then, when my face was still twisted in the clownish fake laugh, and at the exact moment when I felt a bubble of saliva popping at the corner of my mouth, I looked out the bus window and spotted the kid who'd helped Dr. Bratton show me around the school. My Mentor and Big Brother.

I was so glad to see a familiar face that I said "Hi!" as if we were long-lost best friends. Brothers separated at birth. But he was looking at me—*through* me—as if he'd never seen me before.

"Who are *you?*" he said.

"I'm Bart Rangely." How could he not remember?

"Oh, that's right," he said. Now I was beginning to wonder if there was something wrong with *my* memory, if he could have been a different person from the one I'd met on the tour. Could he possibly have a twin brother at the school?

He said, "I'm Tyro Bergen." It seemed less likely that there were two identical guys at the school with the same name. I was still trying to figure out why he didn't recognize me when he said, "I'm supposed to be your . . . Big Brother. Till you get used to this toilet."

I laughed again, as hard as I had when Fat

Freddie had ordered me off the bus, even though Tyro had said "Big Brother" in a way that hadn't sounded like he meant a helpful, loving older sibling, but rather the evil dictator in the George Orwell novel we'd read in seventh grade.

"Big Brother like Big Brother in *1984*?" I said, regretting it instantly.

"What are you talking about?" Tyro said. He turned his back and motioned for me to follow him into the school.

Walking into the main hallway was like diving into the deep end of the pool and not knowing how to swim, like merging with the stream of traffic on a busy highway and having no idea how to drive. The glum nerds who'd ridden the bus with me had disappeared, swallowed up by boys who wore their scratchy blazers and uncool striped ties as if that was the way that everyone should *want* to dress. Boys whose hair shone so brightly it was as if they were wearing mirrors on top of their heads, boys whose confident, loping walks made me understand what it meant when some cheesy book said "Blah-blah *strode* into the room." These guys didn't walk, they strode, like a small private army of teenage gods, and I could tell from the way they treated Tyro that he was their God among gods. Unfortunately, his divinity wasn't exactly wearing off on me, his so-called Little Brother. The other students stared at me the way people look at a stray bug that's turned up someplace where it's especially unexpected or disgusting, a mosquito on an airplane, a cockroach crawling up the wall over your table in a restaurant.

Suddenly I understood what seemed so strange about all this. It wasn't only that Tyro acted as if he didn't recognize me even though you'd think the hours we'd spent on that embarrassing school tour might have been what Dr. Bratton would call a "bonding experience." The weird thing was, I'd gotten used to *everyone* recognizing me, to being our town's version of a local celebrity. Hel-*lo*! I was the Miracle Boy! I was the kid who'd saved his mother from dying on 9/11.

Hadn't any of these guys heard of that? Didn't they read the papers? It crossed my mind that maybe they knew perfectly well who I was, and that they were just pretending not to. Why? So that I would feel like even more of an outsider than I already did.

Every so often, someone would ask Tyro, "Who's the new dude?"

And he would say, "Fart Strangely. I mean Bart Rangely. Fart, this is Buff. This is Pork. This is Dog. This is Ex. Say hi to Fart, guys."

I'd only been at Bullywell for less than five minutes and already I was learning to laugh hysterically at unfunny jokes—jokes on me!

"Hi, Fart," the kids all said. And each time I would think: Thanks, Big Brother. All this time, Tyro kept walking a few steps ahead of me, as if he really were an older sibling annoyed that he had to bring his kid brother along on some fun outing with his friends. By now I was practically skipping to keep up, so that when at last Tyro stopped short outside a classroom door, I had to put on the brakes fast—but I didn't do it fast enough. I plowed right into him.

"Watch it, okay?" he said. "No touching, Fag Face. This is your homeroom, Fart-o. Have fun. Look for me in the lunchroom if you can't find anyone else who can stand to sit with you. Little Bro." And he gave me a friendly push in the direction of the doorway, a push that felt ever so slightly like a nasty shove.

I found myself in a room full of kids who looked like younger, shrunk-down versions of the friends to whom Tyro had so charmingly introduced me. None of these eighth graders had pimples or braces or oily hair or any of the physical defects I'd gotten to know and love among my public school friends. It was as if they'd been born with perfect skin and hair and teeth, and with the promise that, from here on in, things were only going to get better. A funny murmur—not a sound so much as a *feeling*, as if everyone had felt a chill and shivered at once—traveled around the room. I could tell these kids were too young to be very good at pretending not to know who I was. Miracle Boy. The 9/11 semi-orphan. Tragedy Kid. Their new classmate.

I was having such a hard time processing the kids that I didn't even *notice* the teacher until she cleared her throat and said, "Why, hello, Bart. I'm Mrs. Day."

Later, I would learn that everyone called her Mrs. Die, because she looked as if she were just about to. She was positively ancient, though later I began to think that maybe she wasn't as old as she looked, that teaching at Bullywell was one of those experiences, like seeing a ghost or having a loved one die, that turns your hair white overnight. Mrs. Day was so pale she was nearly translucent, as if the light of another world were already shining through her. For a long moment she zoned out, and a film covered her eyes, as if she were gazing into that other world. Then she awoke out of her trance, or whatever it was. Her eyes filled with globby tears and I knew that she recognized me, she knew *exactly* who I was.

73

"Class," she said. "I want you to meet a new student. A very *special* new student."

In a way, it was worse than Tyro introducing me as Fart Strangely. Because the last thing I wanted was to feel more special than I already did.

"Say hello to Bart, class," said Mrs. Day.

"Hello, Bart," they said in an obedient chorus that was like one big group sneer.

"Bart, why don't you take a seat next to Seth?" said Mrs. Day. "Seth, why don't you hold up your hand so Bart will know who you are?"

A set of fingers rose just barely above the heads of the others, and I walked toward the hand to find myself standing over a kid I recognized from the day-student bus. Great! Was this pure coincidence, or had dotty old Mrs. Day sat me next to a fellow loser on purpose?

Actually, Seth *did* have braces and pimples. I guess the reason I hadn't noticed him before was that he slumped so low in his seat that his chin was practically resting on the desk.

"Hi," he said.

"Hi," I said. End of conversation.

It turned out that Mrs. Day was also the English teacher. So we stayed where we were and had English right after homeroom, which at least spared me the nightmare of going back into the hall and rejoining the stream of perfect human specimens masquerading as high school students. To mark the division between homeroom and English class, Mrs. Day said, "All right, gentleman, everybody get up and stretch your legs. Everybody touch your toes and reach up toward the ceiling." No one was going to do *that*! In fact, no one moved, except for a few jocky guys who rolled their shoulders and raised their arms above their heads and cracked their knuckles so loud that the popping sounds seemed to echo off the walls.

"Oh, dear"—Mrs. Day put her hands over her ears—"I do so hate it when you gentlemen do that." Underneath the knuckle popping, Seth— my homeboy, my new fellow-day-student buddy— hissed, "Hey, I saw you walking around with Tyro

Bergen. You *know* him?"

"He's supposed to be my Big Brother," I said. "You know, to help me get used to the school."

"Oh, man," said Seth. "I pity you, dude. He is the baddest of the bad. I mean, he's the meanest of the mean. I'd hate to be your life insurance provider."

"What does that mean?" I asked, stupidly, though I could have figured it out.

Before Seth could answer, if he *was* going to answer, Mrs. Day said, "All right, gentlemen, turn to page thirty-five of *The Great Gatsby*. Let's read aloud, starting from the top of the page."

Everyone groaned and opened their books, except me. Naturally, I didn't have a book. No one had told me to get one. I glanced over at Seth's book, thinking I could look on with him, but he wrapped his elbow around the page, as if he were taking a test and I was trying to copy. I looked up, and Mrs. Day met my eye and grasped my predicament.

"On second thought," she said, "let's take a

little break from poor sad Mr. Gatsby."

Everybody applauded. I hoped they were thanking me for saving them from the boring book! But everyone just moaned again when Mrs. Day said, "Let's all do a little writing exercise. Let's write about . . . hmm. Let's write a little essay about what we did this summer."

"Are you kidding?" someone called out. "We did that the first day of school."

For a moment Mrs. Day looked vaguely alarmed. Then she said, "Let's write about something we didn't mention the first time. Anyway, it'll be nice for Bart. It's a way of getting acquainted. That's *why* we do it the first day of school."

It was clear what Mrs. Day was trying to do— to somehow turn back the clock so that it would be almost as if I was starting the year at the same time as everyone else. I was grateful to her for the effort, but it couldn't have worked. Bullywell had been in session for more than a month before I got there. I felt as if I'd come in on a movie that was already halfway through, so I couldn't understand what was happening on-screen, and some kindly person in the audience was asking the projectionist to rewind the film, for my benefit, and rerun it from the beginning.

Everyone turned to glare at me, as if they wanted their eyes to drill deep, painful holes into my head, as if it were my fault that they were being made to put something down on paper instead of just reading aloud from a book they were supposed to have read. Still grumbling, they took out their notebooks. I tried not to look at anyone, but I could hear a lot of sighing and shifting around, and the sounds of writing and scratching things out and of papers being ripped from their bindings.

I didn't know what to write. I clutched my pen and moved my arm back and forth, scowling at the page as if words were going to appear on it by magic. But of course none did, and the page stayed empty. During the summer, I'd been a counselor-in-training at the town rec program, the same program I'd gone to as a little kid. I guess I could have written about how I'd saved a little girl from drowning. Or maybe she hadn't been drowning, the water wasn't that deep. She'd just gotten freaked and started squealing and I'd had to haul her out.

I could have written about that, but I didn't want to. Because when I thought about the summer, what had really happened was that I came to accept the fact that Dad had traded us in for Caroline. I thought I'd gotten my mind around the fact that he wasn't coming back. Except that I hadn't known what *not coming back* meant. Now I did know, and what had happened to Dad stood, as tall and as terrifying as a building on fire, between me and that glorious day, the pinnacle of my counselor-in-training career, when I'd dragged little Heather, or Molly, or whatever her name was, out of the shallow end of the pool.

After a silence so long I was sure the class would end before anyone got a chance to read his essay, Mrs. Day said, "All right, gentleman, five more minutes." About another hour passed, and then she said, "All right. Time's up. Bart, would you like to go first?"

"I'd rather go last," I said.

For some reason everyone thought this was screamingly funny. When the laughter stopped, Mrs. Day said, "All right. I can respect that. Would someone else like to volunteer?"

One kid—the one whom Tyro had introduced as Ex, which I later learned stood for Extra Credit—read what sounded like a whole novel about how his family had rented a yacht and cruised the Greek islands and every night they snorkeled for octopus and squid (the other kids said "Gross!" and "Yuck!") and the cook who came with the boat would grill the catch over coals on the beach and they'd eat it for dinner. The next kid read about his African safari, another read about his summer house on the Jersey shore. The kid Mrs. Day called on after that said he didn't want to read his, he'd gone to his beach house, too, he'd eaten a ton of lobster, but otherwise his summer was pretty much like that of the kid who'd read before. Meanwhile, I kept thinking that everything anyone read made my richest friends at Hillbrook sound like poor people!

A lot of the pieces were extremely long, which made me realize that, compared to normal teenagers, the students at Bullywell really liked talking about themselves. One kid read for what seemed like twenty minutes about how he saw a bear on his family's otherwise dull trip to some national park. And a lot of the pieces were horribly bad, full of the kind of grammatical mistakes that made me think there were probably lots of spelling errors, too. Until that moment, I hadn't realized that I'd been worried about whether Bullywell might be hard—or "academically challenging," as Dr. Bratton had said—as well as full of vicious bullies. But now I realized that the academic part wasn't going to be the problem.

I'd stopped paying attention, and suddenly I was sweating with dread that Mrs. Day was about to call on me. Then I'd have to confess that I'd just been pretending to write, that there was nothing on the page. I was literally saved by the bell, if you called it being saved to be ejected from my seat in Mrs. Day's uninspiring but harmless classroom and thrown into the churning sea of sharks and barracudas that passed for the halls of Bullywell Prep.

The bizarre thing was, it didn't bother me all that much, because by that point I'd slipped into a kind of fog. All the stuff going on at school seemed amazingly unreal compared to what I was only now starting to see as the hopeless misery of my entire life. If I'd had to find one word for what I was feeling, I guess it would have been: *homesick*. I felt so homesick, it was as if I'd been sent away to live at Bullywell forever and ever. Dude, I told myself, you're a day student. You're going home on the bus tonight. You're going to have dinner with Mom.

Still, it was almost as if the reality of everything that had happened to me—Dad leaving us and then dying in that terrible way—was finally creeping in around the edges of things and making me feel unbelievably lonely and abandoned. When I'd first gotten off the bus, I'd been totally self-conscious, as if I was being watched and judged and sneered at by everyone who saw me. But now I just felt like a big rock stuck in the middle of the school while everything flowed around me. I went to a couple of other classes. I knew what the subjects were: social studies, biology. But that was all I knew. I couldn't understand what anyone was saying.

I was *really* disconnected.

And then at last it was lunchtime, and the dread returned because I could no longer get by just by sitting in class and being silent and passive. I was going to have to find someone to eat with or else face the shame of being that kid in the lunchroom who has to eat all by himself and pretend that he doesn't mind—or that maybe he even *likes* it.

We'd skipped the lunchroom on the school tour we'd taken with Dr. Bratton, and now I understood why. Outside the door was an engraved brass sign that said "Refectory." Paneled in dark wood and decorated with portraits of famous graduates whose expressions of major indigestion seemed like bad advertisements for the food, the lunchroom looked like a banquet hall where some wicked king might serve a lavish feast and poison all the guests. The noise was like rush hour without cars. But the talking and shouting, the clattering dishes and the rattling silverware, and underneath that a smacking sound that I could have sworn was the noise of everyone chewing—all that was nothing compared to the smell: teenage-boy body odor and bad breath and something like spoiled milk, but most of all grease, old grease that had stayed in the air since those guys on the wall used to eat lunch here.

I stood at the entrance, paralyzed, fighting off nausea, telling myself, Dude, the last thing you need is to puke in the lunchroom doorway on your first day at Bullywell.

Just then I heard a soft voice behind me say,

"The food line is over there." I turned to thank my savior, in time to see Seth—the kid from home-room, the geek who wouldn't let me look at his copy of *The Great Gatsby*—scurrying off in the direction he'd indicated. And I thought how much courage it took for Seth to even *talk* to the new kid, and for him to bypass the line on which every-one else was waiting and to join the lonely nerds at a kind of salad bar marked with a big sign that said "Vegetarian Alternative."

I joined the end of the other, presumably non-vegetarian, line, craning my neck so I could see what was being served. I wondered what Bullywell guys *would* eat—raw meat, maybe. I was relieved to see the trays of steamed gray hamburgers and soggy buns. All right! A diet I could handle!

The lunch ladies seemed like twin sisters or clones or at least blood relations of the ones who'd worked at my public school: same hairnets, same tough-gal-with-a-heart-of-gold manner that was basically an invitation to pull out all the stops and be as charming and sweet as you could on the chance—the slim chance—of getting on their good side.

"Burger?" said the one nearest me.

"Thanks," I said, smiling my warmest smile and pretending that I just couldn't inhale enough of that delicious greasy aroma.

She didn't exactly look at me, lunch ladies hardly ever did. But then, almost by accident, she *did* look at me. She paused for a beat, and at first I was confused until I figured out that she'd recognized me from my picture in the papers. Somehow, after just one morning at Bullywell, I'd managed to forget that I was the hero Miracle Boy whom everyone loved and pitied.

"Here," she said. "Take two. You need to keep your strength up. Come back if you're still hungry."

"Thanks!" I practically shouted, embarrassed because tears of gratitude mixed with self-pity had popped into my eyes. It was the first time that anyone had been nice to me all day, not counting Mrs. Day's attempt to make me feel comfortable and Seth offering that helpful little pointer, which was probably just a way to keep me from blocking the lunchroom doorway.

Now that the problem of where to *get* food was solved, I had to face the bigger problem of where I was supposed to eat it. As I stood there with my tray, it was as if I'd become the Invisible Kid. No one saw me, or if they did, they immediately looked away. You'd have thought I was a lunatic who might do something disgusting like sneeze on their plates or grab their food and lick it. Or maybe I had some contagious disease, like leprosy, that they would catch if I sat near them.

Suddenly, I saw someone waving. I turned around because I assumed the person was waving at someone standing behind me. Then I realized it was Tyro Bergen, and that he was waving at *me*, and I remembered his invitation to sit with him at lunch if I couldn't find anyone else to eat with.

His table was surrounded by that special halo that always encircles the coolest kids in school. As I approached, that aura parted for me, and I saw the other guys shifting seats so I could sit next to Tyro. So he was my Big Brother after all. I was already thinking of ways to thank him. Maybe I'd save up all my allowance for the next two years and buy him tickets to a Knicks game in the city.

"Little Bro!" Tyro called. "Come sit your dumb ass over here."

Once more, he introduced me to the guys, some of whom he'd introduced me to before, as Fart Strangely. But that was okay, that was fine with me. Everyone here had a nickname. Maybe after I'd been in school awhile they'd come up with something a little less gross.

The guys—Dog and Pork and Buff—reached over and shook my hand, very grown-up and manly. "Hey, Fart, how ya doin'?" "Whassup?" "How do you like the school?"

"It's great," I said. "It's really great." And at that moment I thought so.

"Whatcha eating, Fart?" said Tyro.

"Two burgers!" one of the guys said. "Fart's got two burgers. What did you do to get *that*, Bart?

Screw the lunch lady?"

"Well," I said apologetically, "maybe it's just because I'm new."

"Because you're new," said Tyro thoughtfully. "Because you're new. . . . That's right, you *are* new. *Very* new, aren't you, Fart. Practically . . . new*born*."

"It's my first day," I said, idiotically. Obviously. Tyro knew that. There was a long silence during which all the guys stared at the two burgers on my plate, and I wished I'd sneaked off and eaten by myself at a distant corner of the refectory. Couldn't *they* get seconds if they wanted? With all the tuition money their parents were paying, you'd think they could have had two measly little burgers. You'd think they could have had twenty!

Finally, just to break the silence, I said, "Could you pass the ketchup?" I didn't like ketchup all that much. But it was something to say.

"Sure," said Tyro. "Ketchup! Coming up! Could you grab the bottle, gentlemen?" The bottle traveled toward me, hand to hand, down the table. I opened it, and shook it, then shook it again. Everyone was watching. I checked to make sure that they hadn't passed me an empty bottle on purpose. This *was* Bullywell, after all. But there was ketchup stuck up in the bottle. It just wasn't moving.

"Stuck ketchup," said Tyro. "It's a Baileywell tradition." Everyone laughed and rolled their eyes as if they knew precisely what he was talking about, as if the worst things they had to put up with at school were gummed-up ketchup bottles. "Want some help with that?"

"Sure," I said, though I had the definite feeling that I didn't.

Tyro took the bottle and, with a single, powerful flick of his wrist, shook it over my burger. Something about the way he did it made him seem like an Olympic athlete performing some brilliant maneuver. A ski jump, a triple axle, a high-speed slalom run.

A modest little blob of ketchup landed dead center on my burger.

"Bull's-eye," said one of Tyro's friends.

"Thanks," I said. "That's great."

Tyro seemed not to hear me. "Want some more?"

"No, that's enough, that's great," I said, but again he acted as if he didn't hear. He gave the bottle another shake, and another plop of ketchup decorated my burger.

"How about some more?" he said.

"No, really," I said. "That's fine."

"But if a little is fine, more is finer, right? More is more, am I correct?" He shook the bottle again. And as I and his friends watched, Tyro shook the bottle again and again. First the burger was swimming in ketchup, then it was drowning in ketchup, and then at last it disappeared beneath a red tide of ketchup. Soon both hamburger buns vanished beneath the spreading red blob, and still Tyro kept shaking the bottle, which by now was nearly empty.

"Gee, man," said the friend Tyro called Buff, and you could see why. "I think something's seriously wrong with your burger."

91

"Roadkill," the one called Dog said.

"I think it's got a bleeding disorder," Pork said. "I think your burger hemorrhaged all over your plate, man."

Everyone laughed.

"That's not funny," Tyro said. "You shut the hell up, Pork."

Everyone shut up. In fact, they lost all interest in me and my burger and my ketchup problem, and went back to talking and eating and laughing as if I weren't there. I stared at the red soup on my plate, until the bell rang and it was time to leave the refectory and go back to class. I was starving.

"Shall we 'do' lunch tomorrow?" Tyro asked me on his way out.

"Yeah," I said. "Absolutely."

Somehow I got through the afternoon. My stomach growled through math class, and a couple of kids snickered. But by then I was too exhausted and sick of it all to care. Instead of going to gym, I had a special getting-to-know-you conference with the assistant gym teacher, Mr. Nevins, who listed all the different team sports and told me to think about which one I wanted to try out for.

"Sure," I said. "I'll think about it. Later." In the back of my mind, I was hoping that the world would end so I wouldn't have to come back to Bullywell ever again.

Then we had after-school art club, led by a woman with long, flyaway blond hair who dressed in robes and beads and who acted like a demented kindergarten teacher. She told us to call her Kristin, and she made us do a "construction," an "autumn piece" that involved pasting crumbs of crispy dead leaves to a sheet of soggy cardboard.

The happiest moment of my entire day came when it was time to get on the loser-day-student bus and go home. In fact, I was so grateful I practically threw myself down on the bus floor in front of Fat Freddie. It took all my self-control not to thank him for saving me from dinner at the refectory and whatever hellish things went on here in the evening after the lights went out.

On the bus, there was an empty seat beside Seth. He didn't smile or do anything friendly, but then again he didn't say I *couldn't* sit there, so I did. You'd think he might have asked, "How did your afternoon go? How was your first day at school?" But he'd apparently missed the lessons Dr. Bratton had referred to, the lessons on how to be a feeling, compassionate leader of the future. Or maybe he already knew how my day had gone. Anyway, I was glad to skip the small talk and get straight to what I really wanted—needed—to know.

I said, "Remember in homeroom you said I should watch out for Tyro Bergen?"

Seth said, "That wasn't me, man. You must be thinking of someone else. I never said any such thing."

"You did," I said. "You *know* you did."

"All right," he said. "Okay. Big deal. I was just stating the obvious. Like saying you should try not to get hit by a truck. Like saying you shouldn't climb the fence at the zoo and sneak into the lion's cage. Like saying—"

"Like saying *what?*" I asked. "What did you mean about Tyro?"

"Nothing."

"Nothing like what?"

"Nothing like . . . Well, okay. Last year he was supposed to be this new kid's Big Brother, and he tortured him so bad that the kid had a total nervous breakdown and dropped out of school before the end of the first term."

"What did he do?"

"I wasn't the guy's psychiatrist, dude. How would I know?"

And then, because in just one day I was already becoming the kind of compassionate underdog-lover that Bullywell aimed to produce, I grabbed Seth's forearm with both hands and twisted his flesh as hard as I could until he said, "Okay! Okay! I think the kid threatened to knock down the bricks at the entrance to the tower and run up and throw himself off the top."

"Moron," I said. "Who cares what *he* did! What I'm asking is, what did *Tyro Bergen* do?"

"Oh, I don't know. No one ever made a big announcement about it, exactly. I guess it because it was so vicious and sadistic."

"So doesn't it seem a little strange to you that, after that, they make him another new kid's Big Brother? Another kid like . . . me?"

Seth said, "I never thought of that." And now, it seemed, he did think about it. After a while, he said, "It was probably his dad's idea. His dad has this big thing about making him a better person. Making all of us better people."

"Yeah," I said. "I feel like a better person already. So what did they do to Tyro after the new kid freaked out and left school?"

Seth looked at me as I'd asked him why day follows night, or why the earth revolves around the sun. "Duh-uh," he said. "Nothing."

"Why not?" I said.

"Because his dad gives a fortune to the school. He owns some kind of bank or something. Or maybe an insurance company. A big corporation, anyway. They're loaded. Tyro gets everything he wants. Dude, haven't you seen his *car*?"

"What car?" I said.

"He's got that white Escalade they let him park in the faculty lot."

"An Escalade? A kid drives an *Escalade*?"

"Come on," said Seth. "You don't think anyone on the faculty could afford a ride like that."

"Dr. Bratton's got a Yukon," I said.

"Bratwurst?" said Seth. "Everybody says that Tyro's dad bought that Yukon for Bratwurst after the trouble Tyro had with the new kid last year. Look, can we stop talking about Tyro? It makes me nervous just to mention the guy."

We rode the rest of the way in silence. When Seth got off the bus, he didn't even say good-bye.

Finally, we got to my stop. There it was—my house! All the lights were blazing. And the truth was, my plain little house had never looked more beautiful than it did that day as we pulled up in front of it.

Just as Dr. Bratton had promised, I got back so late that my mom was already home from her new job, and the house was full of wonderful food smells. If I wasn't mistaken, Mom was making her special pot roast and potatoes. My favorite. Wait until I told Mom that I hadn't even had lunch!

I found her in the kitchen, flushed and happy from cooking. She turned to look at me. I guess she was trying to tell from my face, before I had a chance to say anything, how my first day at school had gone. I tried to arrange my features in the most miserable and sour expression, but the truth was, there was no way I could look glum enough to show her just how much I'd enjoyed my intro-duction to Bullywell.

Our eyes met, and in that instant, I saw how the last month must have looked, from my mom's point of view, the terrible sorrow and confusion of having Dad die so horribly before they could begin to sort things out. I saw what it must have felt like to know that she'd been just a few degrees of fever—my fever—away from dying herself and leaving me to . . . what? To be raised by Gran or one of the aunts? I saw how terrifying it had been for her.

Mostly I saw how desperately she wanted things to be positive and normal, how much she needed me to like my new school, how badly she wanted me to appreciate the privileged education that had come as a gift, a pitiful consolation prize for all that pain and disaster. She wanted me to have the kind of education she thought I'd get at Baileywell. Or maybe she wanted me to get to know rich, powerful people—or, at least, rich kids who would grow up to be powerful people—as if that could somehow protect me and keep me safe. But didn't she know that plenty of rich and powerful people had died, along with Dad, along with weak and poor ones? And didn't she understand that there was nothing safe about Bullywell?

At that moment, I understood that even with the new and better job, the new clothes, even with the satisfaction of firing Caroline, she wasn't a new person. What had happened to Mom—to us both—would never just go away. Life would never be the same for her, she might never completely recover. And the strangest part was, it was as if Dr. Bratwurst was right, as if Baileywell *was* teaching me to see things from the little guy's point of view—maybe not the little guy, but more important, my own mother.

I looked at Mom, and I actually smiled. "It was fine," I said. "I liked it. The kids are really nice. I learned a lot."

For a heartbeat, I worried that maybe I'd laid it on a little too thick. Maybe I shouldn't have added that part about the kids being nice. But Mom didn't seem to notice, or maybe she didn't want to. She hugged me, then pulled back to look at me again, and there were tears in her eyes.

"I'm so happy," she said. "I'm so relieved. Are you hungry? I'm making pot roast."

"I could eat," I said.

CHAPTER FIVE

AND SO BEGAN MY SAD career as one of the bully-ees at Bullywell. Because that was how it broke down: the bullies and the bullied. And though it always took place in secret, totally undercover, you *knew* that it was happening, because it was happening to *you*.

At first I thought I was the only unfortunate victim, but then, from time to time, I'd catch a certain look in someone's eyes, and I'd understand that it was happening to that person, too. After a while, I began to see that there was a system: Every bully had his own personal bully-ee as well as groups of fellow bullies to help with the bullying process. It was as if the school population was divided into little cults or cliques or clubs, each of them based on who was doing the pushing around and who was getting pushed.

Tyro Bergen, my so-called Big Brother, had appointed himself and his friends to be my chief tormentors. At first the incidents were so subtle, I wasn't even sure if they were really happening or if they were just my paranoid fantasies. Did someone purposely dip my tie in the open-faced-turkey-sandwich gravy on the lunch line, or had I done it myself, by mistake? The first time I tripped over someone's foot in the hall and nearly landed on my face and the kid said, "Hey, man, I'm sorry," I sort of believed him. But by the fourth time it happened, I'd stopped believing that it was an innocent mistake. I'd had a silver ballpoint pen I liked that had belonged to my dad. When it disappeared, I honestly didn't know if I'd lost it or if someone had swiped it. I was really sad about that, sadder than I would have imagined. I kept telling myself that I'd lost a pen, not a person. But I *had* lost a person—the person who'd given me the pen. Whenever I thought about that, I'd feel awful all over again. So I tried not to dwell on it.

I suppose I should have been honored, because Tyro was such a star. I should have been flattered that this school celebrity had chosen to torment little me. But of course I wasn't flattered. I was nervous and unhappy and a little—well, more than a little—scared. Because I didn't know how far things would go, how far Tyro would take it, how crazy he was, and what he had in store for me until I gave up and left school or threatened to jump off the tower.

It was almost like we had a relationship. Practically like we were dating, or conducting some insane romance. When I was in the seventh grade I'd had what I guess you could call a crush on a girl named Anna Simonson. I'd find myself thinking about her when I didn't think I was thinking about anything at all. I'd wonder if she was thinking about me. At school I was always superconscious of where she was, superaware when I passed her in the hall or on the stairs. In a strange way, it was like that with me and Tyro. I thought about him semiconstantly, and I wondered if he was thinking about new ways to torment me. Thinking about Tyro occupied as much of my spare time as thinking about Anna Simonson had taken up.

Little by little, the bullying escalated. I knew I should been taking some action. I should have told Mom or one of the more sympathetic teachers, or even sucked it up and gone to Dr. Bratwurst. What did I care about being a snitch? I had something to snitch about! There were important things at stake. My life, for example.

Even if Tyro's dad owned the school and they had to decide between him and me, it was fine with me if they decided to keep him and kick me out on my butt. But I knew that would break my mother's heart even more than it was already broken. She would see it as a huge defeat, and I would feel like a total loser.

Every so often, I'd run into one my old Hillbrook friends, and it was always pretty weird. It felt almost as if they didn't recognize me, or as if they were trying to remember who exactly I was. Maybe they were trying to figure out if I was the same person they used to know, or if I'd turned into one of the Bullywell snobs. One of the Bullywell bullies.

I wanted to say: Hey, look, it's me! It's Bart! We've known each other since the first grade! But that would have been way too embarrassing, and besides, I was starting to wonder if maybe I *wasn't* the same person. I definitely wasn't the Bart they used to know. First I'd turned into Miracle Boy, and now I was a Bullywell bully-ee. Whenever I ran into Mike or Ted or Tim or Josh, or worse, a couple of them together, our conversation was so stiff and awkward that I stopped thinking that going back to Hillbrook—that bully-free para-dise—would solve all my problems. Maybe you could never go back.

Some of the teasing and bullying was harmless, by which I mean physically painless. Still, it was depressing and annoying. Like, for example, the time when someone—Tyro wouldn't have stooped to this, he probably got one of his lackeys to do it for him—put dog shit on the door handle of my locker. I knew that *something* smelled disgusting, but I wasn't looking hard enough or thinking fast enough. Before I knew it, dog shit was all over my hand, which was bad enough, but also all over the cuff of my blazer, which was even worse. I ran to the bathroom and scrubbed and scrubbed, but the odor clung to me and I couldn't get rid of it.

In homeroom, Seth said, "Oh, man, what's the deal? You smell like shit."

I said, "Well, actually, my puppy had a tiny little accident just before I left the house this morning, and I cleaned up after him and—"

"Right," said Seth in a tone that made me think that not only did he know the truth, but I wasn't the first bully-ee at Bullywell to fall victim to the not-exactly-original-or-inspired dog shit–locker trick. Luckily, I had a spare blazer at home, so we could we send this one to the cleaners. I told my mom some story about getting animal waste on my jacket in bio lab.

I felt bad about lying to my mother, but at that point anything seemed better than telling her the truth that would have hurt her, and that would have been so shameful for me. I didn't want her to think she'd raised the kind of kid who'd be singled out to be picked on by the other kids. The fact was, I kept telling myself, I *wasn't* that kind of kid. I was just a kid who'd been unlucky enough to be sent to the wrong school at the wrong time.

By my second week at Bullywell, it was clear that my nickname was going to stick. Every time I walked down the hall, someone would aim lip farts in my direction, and some days I'd hear a whole chorus of them. Everyone called me Fart Strangely, and even the kids who, I could tell, were trying to be halfway nice, would say, "Hey, Fart, I mean Bart." So that became my second nickname: Fart I Mean Bart. That's what Tyro called me sometimes. Fart. I. Mean. Bart. He'd say it very slowly, threateningly, as if every word was a promise of something I wasn't going to like, something dangerous and unpleasant.

Every so often my mom would ask, "Have you made any new friends at school?"

And I would say, "Well, there's this one kid, Seth. But he lives pretty far away."

Though Seth and I sat together sometimes on the bus, and we had neighboring seats in homeroom and English, our conversation had never gotten friendly or personal enough for us to exchange addresses. All I knew was that the bus dropped Seth off about fifteen minutes before me. Once my mother said, "What about that boy— what was it, Tycho or Tyrone—who came with us on the school tour? He seemed so friendly and nice. So good-looking, too."

I felt a kind of funny flutter, almost like an extra heartbeat, when I said, "Yeah, well, he is pretty nice. I guess. But we don't hang out that much with the older kids."

I could tell my mother was worried about my not having made new friends, so in a way it was almost helpful when the phone calls started coming. The first couple times I let my mom answer because I was sure the call wasn't for me. She'd turned to me with a puzzled expression, saying it must have been a wrong number. The caller had hung up.

After that I ran for the phone, saying, "It's probably for me!" Because you could say it *was* for me, I knew it was for me, though not in the way people generally understand that phrase: *for me*. I'd answer and hear someone breathing and sometimes a few giggles or snorts in the background as I said *"Hello? Hello?"* And I'd hear my own voice coming back at me like a shout echoing down a well.

Eventually I figured out how to make it work for me. Whenever the phone rang, I would answer and listen to the silence for a while, and then I'd press my finger down on the button and pretend to talk, loud enough for my mom to hear. I acted as if I was talking to whoever she imagined my new friends were. It was strange, having these conversations about school and homework and life in general with the dial tone, but it was worth it, because when I came back into the living room after talking to my pretend friends, I could see the worry lines smoothing out of my mother's face.

Every so often, I would catch myself thinking: As bad as this is, it's the calm before the storm. I'll look back on this as the good time. I understood that I was enjoying a temporary reprieve, waiting for the bullying to get worse. I could tell that Tyro and his friends were already getting bored with this low-level harassment, and I sensed that they were figuring out how to take it to the next level. What exactly would they do to me to re-create the success they'd had last year with the kid who threatened to throw himself screaming off the tower?

It was a Saturday, in early November. When I was really little, I used to watch cartoons on TV every

Saturday morning with Mom, just the two of us waiting for Dad to wake up, because he liked to sleep in. Years had passed since then, but we'd kept up the habit. Now we watched Japanese anime, and Mom didn't notice the difference, she didn't seem to care that it was no longer Inspector Gadget. I think she just liked the ritual of spending that time with me.

It was embarrassing to be thirteen and still watching cartoons with your mom, and I wondered if when I grew up and left home and had a house of my own, Mom would still expect me to come home every Saturday morning. At the same time, it felt good, it was comforting. Though I never would have told anyone, the truth was I really liked snuggling up next to Mom on the couch as the bright flashing images chased each other across the screen.

Pokémon had just started when the phone rang.

"It's probably for you," Mom said. "I talked to Gran and Aunt Grace earlier this morning."

I was already out the living room door. I picked up the phone in the kitchen. Silence. Breathing. In the background, a TV was playing, and I listened, vaguely curious as to whether they were watching the same program we were. I was just about to hang up when I heard a voice—it was Tyro's voice, he didn't even try to disguise it—say, "How would you like to die, Fart?"

"Not much," I said. "Actually, not at all." Then I hung up the phone and just stood there, staring at the receiver. I didn't really believe that Tyro was going to kill me. But it was a message, a signal that a new offensive had begun, that the brief truce—or whatever it was—had ended.

Suddenly it crossed my mind: Maybe he *did* mean to kill me. Oddly enough, I wasn't all that scared, though I knew that if Tyro and his friends decided to murder me, they'd probably choose some slow and painful torture. The worst part was imagining how my mom would feel after it happened, on top of what had happened to my dad and everything else she'd been through. It made me never want to go to school again. And yet I was afraid that if I faked it and stayed home without being sick, it would be bad luck and undo all the good luck (if you could call it good luck) I'd gotten that September morning by staying home when I was *really* sick.

I went back into the living room. My mom was glued to the TV watching some skinny Japanese kid ride a snorting dragon into a kung fu–style fight with some kind of demon.

"Who was that?" asked Mom.

"Oh, just a friend from school," I said.

"Glad to hear it," said Mom. "It makes me happy to know that you're doing so well." And once again I felt as if I were having that old dream in which someone was about to hurt me and my parents couldn't save me. But now it was only Mom, and she certainly couldn't help. She didn't seem to have the slightest suspicion that I was in danger.

CHAPTER SIX

SOMETIMES YOU HEAR people talk about waiting for the other shoe to drop. And that was what I was doing. Waiting for the other shoe to drop—on my head. I could feel the pressure building as we neared the Thanksgiving vacation. It was as if Tyro and his friends wanted to do something major—something to me—that would make them feel they'd earned the right to kick back with their family and friends and gorge themselves on turkey and all the trimmings.

I was careful, I watched my back, I felt like

were, had gone away. Or so I thought. But I was wrong. Because after a few minutes, I heard someone speaking through the grate.

Tyro said, "If you tell anyone who did this, I promise—no, I *swear*—we'll kill you."

And then they were finally gone. I waited for a few minutes, and then—when I knew I couldn't stand the dark and the closed-in, suffocating feeling one more second—I began to bang on the locker door. I banged and shouted for a very long time. Maybe everyone was in class. No one heard me, or if they did, they pretended not to. Suddenly I got really scared. Maybe there had been a bomb scare or something—like there had been a few times in public school—and everyone had left the building. I even worried that they'd all gone home for the day and I would be stuck there all night, though I knew that wasn't possible. Only a few minutes had passed since school started, and it was still early morning. Still, I kept banging and banging and calling out, *"Help, help!"* though it was *highly* embarrassing to be calling out like that.

It felt like one of those dreams in which you try to run or yell and you can't move, or maybe you can move your mouth, but no sound comes out, and no one hears you.

Finally I heard voices outside the locker. I prayed that it wasn't Tyro and his friends coming back to see if I'd suffocated yet, or gone crazy. To see if their attempted murder or whatever had succeeded.

Someone called out, "What's your combination number?" And amazingly, I remembered. I could tell that someone was fiddling with the lock, and after a while the lock clicked open.

Light and air flooded in. It took several minutes for my eyes to adjust to the dazzle. Then I saw the school security guard, and behind him a group of teachers, and then Dr. Bratwurst's big face, looking way more frightened even than I probably looked, as he asked, "Are you all right? Are you all right?"

"Sure," I said. "I'm fine. I don't know what happened."

That's what I kept saying. I didn't know what happened. Someone grabbed me from behind and hit me and stuffed me into the locker before I could see who it was. I didn't mention the warning that Tyro had whispered through the slots. No one asked if anyone had said anything to me once I was locked inside. Anyway, there had been something in his voice that made me half—well, a quarter—believe him when he said they'd kill me if I told.

First they had the nurse check me over and write up a detailed report, just in case I decided to sue the school or something. But there was nothing much for her to write. No bones were broken, no teeth lost. I did get a few ugly bruises, but they didn't come out until the next day, and by then I certainly wasn't about to go back to the nurse and tell her to add that to the report.

After the nurse got through with me, Dr. Bratwurst called me into his office. He asked if anything like that had happened to me before. I said no, and it wasn't exactly a lie. *Some* things had happened, but nothing quite like *that*. It was a strange conversation, because everything was punctuated by long silences, during which I looked over at his computer, at the screen saver of tropical fish gliding back and forth in the turquoise ocean.

By this time, I'd calmed down enough to wonder why Dr. Bratwurst was making such a big deal about this. After all, Bullyville was famous for this sort of thing. Compared to some kid nearly jumping off the tower, my being stuffed in a locker didn't seem so bad. But then I began to wonder if his concern had something to do with the way it would look if it got out—let's say, if me or my mom happened to tell a reporter—that Miracle Boy was being tortured by his new friends at Baileywell Prep.

After a lot of throat-clearing and hesitation, Dr. Bratwurst suggested that my mom might want to come in for a conference, so he could personally assure her that this wouldn't happen again.

I said, "Well, actually, no, she probably doesn't."

I asked him if we could please not bother her with this, because she'd been through so much lately. I was basically playing the Dad card, and it worked. When Dr. Bratwurst looked at me, he seemed to be on the edge of tears. He also seemed relieved when he said, "Fine, then, let's spare your mother the pain of dealing with this little . . . incident. I'm sure it's a one-time occurrence and that it won't be repeated."

I said, "I certainly hope so."

Dr. Bratwurst said, "My sense is that all this will probably end right here."

I said, "I hope that, too."

But of course it didn't.

A few days before Thanksgiving, Dr. Bratwurst announced that the traditional holiday assembly was canceled, so we could forget about the Thanksgiving hymns we'd been practicing in music class for weeks. No "All Things Bright and

Beautiful." No "A Mighty Fortress Is Our God. Ex—that is, Extra Credit—took it really hard, because he'd written a really long, skin-crawlingly creepy poem called "The Gifts of the Pilgrims" that Mrs. Day had arranged for him to read aloud to the whole school.

Instead of all that fun entertainment, Dr. Bratwurst walked solemnly up to the podium. As the portrait of yet another old geezer—in this case, Governor Bailey, the founder of Bullywell and supposedly the discoverer of Bailey Mountain—peered down over his shoulder, Dr. Bratwurst took off his glasses as if he meant to gaze deeply into all our eyes—all our souls—at once. He gave his tie a meaningful tweak and said, "It has recently come to my attention that there have been incidents of what I suppose is called hazing or . . . bullying . . . at Baileywell."

It had *recently* come to his attention? Was he the only person on the planet that didn't know the school was called Bullywell? Meanwhile, I couldn't help noticing that he'd said "incidents." Plural.

"And it grieves me," he said. "It grieves me more deeply than I can tell you, gentlemen. Because our mission here is to turn out not just students with a grasp of the academic disciplines, not just leaders who will take the reigns of tomorrow's society in hand, not just men who can raise families and sustain friendships and do good in the world. Not just men like that but also . . . compassionate, caring human beings. Men with sympathy for the underdog, big men who can see things from the little guy's point of view. And to bully a fellow creature, to pick on someone weaker and smaller than you are . . ."

I didn't exactly like the "weaker and smaller part," but there was nothing I could do about it, and besides, Dr. Bratwurst meant well, even though his well-meaning little speech was not going to make the tiniest bit of difference. Anyway, I was only half listening to what Dr. Bratwurst was saying because half of me—maybe more than half of me—was thinking about Tyro, wondering where he was sitting. As much as I would have liked to, I was afraid to turn around and look for him. I was afraid that his eyes might meet mine by accident—and then what would I do? I wondered what he was thinking, if he thought I'd told Dr. Bratwurst that he and his friends were responsible for my having been shut up in the locker.

Was Tyro dreaming up some cruel way to kill me, as he'd threatened, for telling? I reminded myself that this wasn't my fault. It was Tyro's fault, he'd started it. And beyond that, it was the fault of the terrorists who'd flown into the building and killed my dad and set off the chain of events that was responsible for my having wound up at this school. But that just made my present situation seem even *more* like Tyro's fault. To pick on someone like me, after what had happened to me, made it seem as if he couldn't possibly have a heart.

Or maybe I just thought that because Dr. Bratwurst kept saying "heart." "Not just intellect but heart," he said, "not just courage but heart, not just originality but heart. That's the kind of young men we want Baileywell to produce. Men with *heart*. And that's what I want you think about. Over this break, when you're with your family and your loved ones, while you're eating your turkey dinner and, more important, as you're giving thanks for all that you have and for how much more fortunate we are than so many others. I want you to think about *heart*, and about how to make your heart the very center of your being, your ultimate authority, your commander in chief."

At some point during all of this I got sort of stuck on the idea of turkey hearts—and that little package of disgusting innards that, one Thanksgiving, Mom forgot to take out of the bird. It pretty much ruined the dinner, and Dad got really mad. The thought was distracting, and it was keeping me from following where Dr. Bratwurst was taking this.

"On a more practical note," he was saying, "we're not—not *yet*—going to ask the students responsible for this unforgivable behavior to turn themselves in. But let me tell you, let me assure you . . . no, let me *warn* you, that the entire staff and faculty and administration of Baileywell and I myself will be, from now on, so to speak, on high alert. Red alert. Any further incident of this kind will be dealt with promptly and punished with the utmost severity. And with zero tolerance."

I sort of liked the sound of that until I remembered what Seth had said about Tyro's father more or less owning the school, so that they wouldn't punish him no matter what he did.

"All right, then Baileywellers," said Dr. Bratwurst. "Have a happy, healthy holiday."

The whole student body began to applaud, and the applause got louder and louder until it became a kind of roar. Then one person got up, and another, and then everyone rose and exploded out of the auditorium and into the halls and out of the building and into the arms of their happy, healthy, rich, intact two-parent families.

CHAPTER SEVEN

I T WAS GREAT TO BE out of school for a few days, to be able to get up in the morning without being afraid that by the end of the day I would be stuffed in my locker or tortured or terrorized or dead. On the other hand, I wasn't exactly looking forward to Thanksgiving.

As usual, we were having dinner at Gran's house, with all the aunts and uncles and cousins. I'd always liked holidays with my mom's family. It was sort of like spending time with a bunch of very talkative, affectionate octopuses. Arms and hands everywhere, everyone kissing and hugging, everyone eating and laughing and talking with their hands and reaching out to touch you when they wanted to make some kind of point that you could never hear anyway, because everyone was talking at once.

I also liked the fact that even though everyone got older—especially me and my cousins—nothing ever changed. Sooner or later, Aunt Grace, who talked in that strange British accent, always got into some kind of argument with Aunt Barb. Aunt Faye's husband, Joe, always drank too much wine and said something really stupid, and Aunt Barb's husband always insisted on watching the football game on TV and fell asleep in front of it. Then someone waded into the fight between whatever aunts were arguing until finally Gran put her hands over her ears and said, Stop, stop, she couldn't stand it anymore, and everyone stopped.

Plus my cousins were fun: The little ones were cute and the older ones always had some trick up their sleeves. Once, at Christmas, when I was really small, my cousin Steve took me outside and gave me a cigarette to smoke and I came back inside and vomited all over Gran's table. And once, when I wasn't much older than that, my cousin Suzanne painted my fingernails purple, and everyone laughed, except for my uncle Ernie, who for some reason bopped my gay cousin Billy—who'd had nothing to with it—on the side of the head.

But this year, when everything else was going so terribly wrong, it made sense that not even Thanksgiving could come without its own ready-made problem looming on the horizon.

About two weeks before the holiday, Mom informed me that she was inviting a guest to Gran's Thanksgiving. I didn't like the way she said "guest."

"Who?" I asked.

"A guy from work." I liked the way she said "guy from work" even less than I'd liked "guest."

"What's his name?" I asked.

"Bernie," she said.

"You're inviting a guy named *Bernie*? *Bernie?*"
It *was* a dorky name, but obviously the name wasn't
what was bothering me

"Actually, everyone calls him Bern," said
Mom, which made me feel worse. Mom hadn't
been at her new job all that long, and she already
knew this dork well enough to be calling him
Bern? It was all I could do not to make a really
vicious, stupid joke and say something mean and
hurtful, like "Burn? That's what happened to Dad,
isn't it?"

That's how freaked I was. Because I was suddenly afraid that this Bern was Mom's new
boyfriend or maybe tryout boyfriend or wannabe
boyfriend, and it didn't seem right. Dad had only
been dead for two months. But if you counted the
six months before that, I mean the six months
since he'd left us, and if you factored in Caroline,
well, that changed the equation, too. I didn't care.
I didn't want Mom to have a boyfriend. I couldn't
handle any more changes.

I didn't know what to say, or if I had a right to say anything at all. But what I couldn't help saying was, "Is Bern your new boyfriend or something?"

"It's not like that, sweetie," said Mom. "It's not like that at all. Bern's wife died this summer. Of cancer. He has no kids, his family lives in California, and he has no one to spend Thanksgiving with. It just seemed like a kind thing to do. A simple good deed. And you know, something about what happened to us, and what happened to all those families . . . it just makes you want to be extra caring and extra kind to people."

I stared at Mom. It wasn't like her to say things like "extra caring" and "extra kind"; it seemed like just one more sign of how much she'd changed. Well, of course she'd changed. I'd changed, too. The whole world had changed. And it *did* make you want to be a nicer, extra kind person. I just couldn't help wondering why it didn't have that same effect on Tyro.

"All right," I said. "Fine. Go ahead. Invite this *Bern* dude if you absolutely *have* to." Meanwhile I was thinking: Definitely the tryout boyfriend. Mom's trying him out on me and the rest of the family. Go ahead and ruin Thanksgiving, Mom. Who cared? This Thanksgiving was pretty much ruined in advance, what with all we'd gone through, and everything that had happened, and the fact that not just us but everyone in the country seemed to be still waiting for the other shoe to drop.

I loved the feeling of walking into Gran's house on Thanksgiving. It was always warm, too warm, and it always smelled awesome. It smelled like turkey, of course, but mixed with the other dishes: pasta and meatballs, eggplant parmesan, fried calamari—all sorts of delicious food that Gran could never get through her head weren't part of your typical basic American Thanksgiving.

We were a little late. Mom was bringing her special Brussels sprouts and chestnut casserole and a green salad, and we were halfway to Gran's when she remembered she'd forgotten the vinaigrette, and we had to go all the way home and get it. So most of the family was already there, and everyone swarmed all over us, hugging and kissing us, telling me how much I'd grown, telling Mom how pretty she looked. In other words, the usual.

But this year I couldn't help thinking that they were hugging and kissing me twice as much, or maybe the hugs were just lasting twice as long, because I was the poor pitiful orphan whose dad had been killed, and also the Miracle Boy who had saved their beloved daughter and sister and sister-in-law and aunt—that is, Mom—from the same terrible fate.

It was positively weird how everyone was on their best behavior, trying to avoid the usual arguments. And how everyone was treating Mom and me as if we were as fragile as Gran's shepherd and shepherdess figurines, delicate china statues that, we were always told, would break if we looked at them too hard. Every so often, tears would pop into Gran's eyes, or one of the aunts would reach in her purse for a Kleenex, and I'd know that they were thinking about Dad, maybe thinking that this was the first Thanksgiving, the first holiday, without him. I half wanted to tell them that Dad might not have been here even if he were still alive. He might have been celebrating with Caroline. But I couldn't see how that would help. It would only make everything more confusing, and worse for Mom and me.

Even so, it was all good. In fact, I was sort of happy, because after all those days of feeling despised and excluded at Bullywell, it was great to be around people who knew me, who'd known me since I was born. And who liked me—well, actually, they *loved* me. I concentrated really hard, as if my brain were a video camera that could somehow record everything that my family was saying and doing. Then I could play the tape back to myself during the next bad time at Bullywell, which, I was pretty sure, would begin the minute school started again. I tried not to think about Bullywell, and just to enjoy the moment. And it would have been one hundred percent perfect if I hadn't noticed that Mom kept glancing nervously toward the door.

Great, I thought. She's waiting for Bern to arrive.

Every time Mom looked toward the door, everyone else did, too. I could tell they were wondering who this guy, this *Bern*, was, wondering whether he was the replacement husband, the replacement dad, and wondering whether it wasn't a little *soon* after the real dad had been killed to start thinking about a replacement.

Finally the doorbell rang. I took one look at the guy who walked in, and I thought: Mom must be really desperate or else her taste has gone drastically downhill since Dad. Dad had been confident and good-looking, but Bern looked like the nerds I rode to school with on the day-student bus. He wore glasses, and he was bald but for a little tuft of fluffy hair growing out of the top of his forehead. Not only did he have no chin but he was *so* chinless that the bottom of his face seemed to be attached directly to his neck.

When Mom greeted him and introduced him to all the relatives, he looked up only briefly, as if he were afraid that any contact with another human being might interrupt whatever serious communication he was having with his own feet. When Mom introduced him to me, he checked me out for a second or two, not long or carefully enough for me to even imagine that he was looking over a kid who might be a part of his future. So, in a way, I could begin to take it easy. This certainly wasn't my future dad. It occurred to me that Mom was actually doing what she'd said— being kind to a sad guy who would otherwise have spent Thanksgiving all alone. And I could tell that Gran and the aunts and uncles were coming to the same conclusion at the same time, so everyone could just relax around the whole Bern question.

Even so, there was something about Bern's presence—maybe it was the fact of his being a stranger in a house where everyone else was family—that made me nervous. And I had the definite feeling that Bern had the same effect on everyone, even my youngest cousins. We were all jumping out of our skins. Everyone shook hands awkwardly except for Gran, who threw her arms around Bern and kissed him on both cheeks, and then for some reason everyone laughed and for a few moments the mood lightened.

In a way, I thought, there was something good about Bern's having been invited. He was sort of a distraction. Without this creepy stranger here for us to focus on, we might have been even more aware of—even sadder about—Dad's absence. And maybe Mom had known that, too.

Still, something about Bern really bothered me, but I couldn't figure out what it was. He was given the guest-of-honor seat next to Gran. He mumbled please and thank you when the dishes were passed his way. When Uncle Ernie carved the turkey, Bern said, "Only a little white meat for me, please."

Everyone looked at everyone else. *Only a little white meat, please?*

139

In fact, Bern took only small portions of every-thing—which was so totally un-Thanksgivinglike, he could have been celebrating a different holiday than the rest of us. As we loaded our plates and tucked into our meal, Bern lowered his head so near his food that he hardly had to use a fork to lift that scrap of white meat to his mouth. He could have just scarfed it up directly off the dish.

Gran and a couple of the aunts tried to strike up conversations with him. "So, Bern, I hear you work with Corinne." "How long have you worked with Corinne, Bern?" How long *could* Bern have worked with Corinne? Most everyone who used to work with Corinne before September was dead. Anyway, Old Bern could only spare one syllable at a time—"Yes, two weeks"—lest anything get in the way of the teensy, pleasureless bites he was tak-ing, one after another; lest anything interrupt his chewing very slowly and methodically, as if he were scared of choking. Bern took a morsel of stuffing, a dab of potatoes, a mini-taste of Gran's meatballs and lasagna. And then, amazingly, Bern opened his mouth and spoke.

"What was that?" asked Uncle Dan.

Mumble mumble mumble.

"Excuse me?" said Aunt Barb.

Bern said, "Do you have any ketchup?"

Ketchup? At Thanksgiving? Hadn't this guy ever heard of gravy and cranberry sauce? But what the hell, Bern was the guest. Mom started to get up, but Aunt Grace practically shoved her back into her chair, and returned from the kitchen with a bottle of ketchup, all crusted over as if it had been in the refrigerator for about thirty years. Bern shook it and shook it and then a watery stream emerged. It looked as if someone had been bleeding onto his turkey. And all at once I had the shameful desire to do to Bern what Tyro had done to me, that first day at Bullywell, to shake ketchup all over his food until his plate was a sea of red.

All at once, I knew what bothered me so much about Bern. He didn't just remind me of the geeks I rode to school with. He reminded me of *me*. He reminded me of me at school, the person I became as soon as I walked in the front door of Bullywell Prep. No one knew him, no one liked him, no one knew anything about him, and at the end of the day, no one would.

I knew that should have made me feel sympathy for Bern, who was suffering, like me. But the truth was, it made me hate him. It made me wish he would just get up and leave Gran's house immediately. So I guessed I wasn't becoming the kind of person Dr. Bratwurst wanted us to become—full of compassion and heart. Whatever was happening to me at school seemed to be hardening my heart instead of softening it, shrinking it instead of making it larger. I couldn't stop thinking about that, couldn't stop feeling my heart clench and grow smaller inside me. And somehow that made me sadder than anything else. I *had* changed, I had *really* changed. And not for the better.

Then I thought of Tyro, and I wondered about *his* Thanksgiving. I imagined silver and fine china and a gleaming mahogany table surrounded by super-uptight, superrich relatives not talking to each other except to say, Pass the canned peas, Pass the skim milk, Pass the white bread. Maybe he had a rotten family, maybe that was why he was so mean to me. There had to be some explanation. But I didn't know that for sure. All I knew was that his dad had tons of money. Maybe his family was wealthy *and* loving and warm, maybe he tortured me for me no reason except that he liked the feeling of making other people miserable, and he could do it and could get away with it and not have to pay the price.

Less than five minutes after the coffee cups were cleared, Bern thanked everyone and excused himself and left. It seemed to me that everyone heaved a huge sigh of relief.

"What a nice young man," said Gran.

"What a tragedy," said Aunt Faye, "to lose your wife like that and not have kids or anyone to spend the holidays with." And then everyone fell silent, and I knew they were all thinking of what had happened to Mom and me, though of course they didn't know the true story, and they probably never would.

Meanwhile, I was realizing that all the time Bern had been there, I—and everyone else—had been afraid that he was going to break down and burst into tears and weep into his white-meat turkey. The minute he was gone, we became the Octopus Family again, everyone reaching and gabbing and touching one another. The same arguments broke out, someone turned on the television, and the football game started.

My cousin Brian sidled up to me and asked in a whisper if I wanted to step outside and smoke some weed, but I said, No, thank you, I'm fine. The storm cloud of Bern had gathered and passed. Things were cool. And for the moment, I *was* fine.

CHAPTER EIGHT

SCHOOL STARTED AGAIN, and now we were in that narrow window of time between Thanksgiving and Christmas through which you can see a faint ray of light at the end of the tunnel. It made me think of those winter afternoons when it suddenly gets dark and you're walking home alone and you're scared and you first see your house, and maybe your mom at the window. All I had to do was survive for a couple of weeks, and then school would let out for the long vacation.

Bullywell Christmas break was about twice as

long as the public school's, I guess so all the Bullywell families could jet off to their magnificent ski lodges in Switzerland and Aspen. When I was still in public school, kids used to say that the insanely long winter break was the only reason why anyone might ever want to go to Bullywell. But now, knowing what I knew, I wouldn't have gone there if vacation had lasted the rest of the year. Anyway, Mom and I weren't planning to go anywhere for Christmas.

By the time we all got back to school after Thanksgiving, Dr. Bratwurst had hired a couple of hall monitors to keep on eye on the bullying and "harassment" incidents, to keep things under control. But something about the guys he'd found wasn't exactly reassuring. They looked like secret-service men who'd been fired for letting the important official they were protecting get assassinated, and they didn't seem any too overjoyed about their demotion. They still dressed like spies or CIA ops, they wore dark glasses even indoors and those creepy short haircuts. In their dark blue blazers they looked like guys who might have graduated at the bottom of their class at Bullywell, and wound up back at their old school. They'd probably failed everything and still gotten an A plus in Bullying 101, the subject Bullywell taught best. They'd be more likely to join the bully than to stick up for the kid getting beaten up.

But even that was okay, because I seemed to have lucked into another one of those temporary reprieves. Tyro hardly even gave me a second glance when we passed in the hall. He seemed not to recognize me. Likewise, his friends acted like they'd never met me before. Maybe they'd taken Dr. Bratwurst's warning seriously, and they were worried about being caught and maybe (with the exception of Tyro, of course) expelled. But I was pretty sure I hadn't gotten *that* lucky. It was more likely that they'd retreated once again to regroup and come up with some plan to torture me in a way that was worse than anything they'd done before, to do something really horrible for which they *couldn't* get caught. Nothing happened.

Nothing happened. And then more nothing happened. Everything felt suspended, underwater, waiting.

One morning, between English class and social studies, I was walking down the hall, and I got a text message. I never got calls in school, we weren't allowed to. Just having your phone ring in class—even if you didn't take the call—meant automatic detention.

But that morning, for some reason, I'd left the phone on. I didn't even look at the number to see who was calling. I assumed it was Mom. These days, she was the only person who ever called me on my cell. Sometimes she'd just text-message me to say, "Hi, it's me, I love you."

And that's what it said, "Hi, it's me." I smiled, thinking of Mom. And it made me a little less nervous as I walked down a hall crowded with kids who seemed not to see me and into a class with a teacher who didn't seem to like me much, either.

A few seconds later, the phone vibrated again. And the message said, "It's hot." Maybe it wasn't

Mom. Mom never talked about the weather. She said it was boring to talk about the weather. And now that I thought about it, Mom never text-messaged me about anything except to say that she loved me.

Still, the next time the phone buzzed, I checked the message.

Okay, here's the truth. It's embarrassing, but there's no other way to explain why I kept check-ing the phone. The fact was, I wouldn't have paid it any attention if I hadn't just read an article in the newspaper about how they'd recently discov-ered some new way to download porn sites onto your phone. So I was sort of wondering if they'd found out my number, and if this was a test run. What else could "It's hot" mean?

A few seconds passed. The phone vibrated again. The letters spelled out, "It's very hot." Okay, fine, I'd stay with it long enough to see where all this was going. I had a few minutes before class. Another message came in. All right, let's give this one last chance. Then I had to bounce.

This time the message was longer, and I watched the letters spell out: "It's hot. It's very hot. It's burning hot. I'm burning up. Love, Dad."

It took me a weirdly long time to understand what I was reading. And the strangest thing was that, for a few minutes, I believed it. I thought it really *was* a message from Dad, because Dad used to text-message me all the time. Even after he moved in with Caroline, he'd still send messages telling me he loved me and asking how I was doing, but mostly I didn't answer, because I was so mad at him for leaving us. That's what I thought about now, how guilty I felt for not having answered all those messages when now I'd never have the chance to message him back and ask how *he* was doing and when he was coming home. And to tell him I loved him, too.

Everything seemed be happening in slow motion. So slow that it seemed to take me about an hour to realize that of course it wasn't Dad. It couldn't have been Dad. My dad was dead. Someone wanted me to feel as bad as I could, though of course whoever it was couldn't know how bad I felt. No one could imagine. Then it all came pouring in on me at once: missing Dad and being in this terrible place where someone—for no reason, and not because of anything I could have done to him—someone wanted me to be in as much pain as it was possible to feel and still be walking and talking.

And then finally it was too much, way too much. I couldn't take any more. I looked around, took a quick left turn, bypassed the social studies classroom, and headed for the boys' bathroom. And maybe there really *were* miracles, because by some miracle no one was in there to see me or hear me. I went into one of the stalls and burst into heaving, choking sobs. I was crying for myself, and for Dad, and for everything I'd lost, and for how lonely and scared I was, and how I couldn't tell anyone, and how no one could help me. Or even understand.

I washed my face. I pulled it together. But I never went to social studies class. I thought: If anyone asks, I'll tell them I had some kind of stomach attack. Maybe I should go to the nurse and stay there until school lets out. I could fake it, I knew. By now my face was all streaked and swollen from crying. I could tell the nurse that the stomach cramps were so bad they'd made me cry.

I waited in the bathroom, all alone, feeling sorrier and sorrier for myself. But the thing is, even at the worst times, there's only so long you can pity yourself. And after a while, my sadness began to change. It was almost if someone had lit a fire under all that grief, and it was heating up, simmering, and then boiling over into anger.

Rage, actually. What I felt was rage, pure rage. I wanted to hurt someone, I wanted to kill someone, I wanted revenge for everything that had been done to me. I would have liked to get the guys who flew into the towers, but they were already dead, so I'd take the nearest substitutes: Tyro Bergen and his friends. They'd do fine to take revenge on. What the bullies were doing to me was as pointless and heartless and cruel as flying an airplane into a building and killing all those innocent people.

I knew I couldn't kill Tyro and the others, even if I'd wanted to. I couldn't even beat them up. I was way outnumbered. I had no allies, no backup. Besides, no matter how mad I was, I knew I could never kill anyone, ever. I had to think of something else.

And then I did.

I hid in the bathroom till lunch period, when everyone was occupied, busy waiting on the lunch line and chewing and swallowing and yelling and pouring ketchup all over some other kid's burger. Then I sneaked outside. I was a little worried that the secret-service hall monitors might catch me, but they must have taken a lunch break, too. They weren't anywhere around. I went down the stairs and out the door to the parking lot. And now I really was lucky. The gods—and maybe there *were* gods of justice, or at least revenge—must have been on my side, because the parking lot was empty.

I recognized Tyro's car right away. The big

white Escalade stood out from the Toyotas and Hondas the teachers drove, as if it belonged to a whole different species. Even Dr. Bratwurst's Yukon looked puny beside it.

For a few minutes I stood there, motionless, in front of Tyro's Escalade. I had to get over the eerie feeling that the headlights and the grille were looking at me, that they somehow knew what I was going to do. I felt like myself and not myself. Like someone else. Like an actor in a movie. I even knew the name of the film: *Miracle Boy's Revenge*. And the way I knew what do next was that I'd seen it in so many films.

I took my house keys out of my pocket and dragged them along the side of the car door, scratching off some paint. The first time, I was hesitant, almost gentle. The groove didn't go very deep, not because I was afraid to dig in, but because some part of me didn't believe that it would actually work.

It worked, all right. There was a thin little scratch where there hadn't been a scratch before.

I stood back. I liked the way it looked. I liked it so much that I did it again. This time I made another scratch, deeper and longer. I came at it from a different angle, and with the third scratch I made an X, like spindly telephone wires crossing the snowy field of the white car.

It was fun, in a way. I liked it. I knew it wasn't a great thing to do. A *compassionate* thing to do. But I enjoyed every scratch I made. I went around to the front of the car, and I felt like a painter who's just gotten a huge new canvas. Okay, let's see what I could accomplish here. I had to stretch and lean way over for this one, but I made a deep, hard, jagged groove all the way across the hood. Then another and another, then a sort of zigzag.

I kept looking over my shoulder. I was still expecting to get caught. My heart kept skipping beats. But then I stopped worrying about that. And after a while I began to feel, inside my chest, a whole different kind of heartbeat. Musical and kind of trippy, as if a dancer deep inside me were doing a fast, superjoyous salsa.

Still, my little art project didn't feel finished. So I began to write. I wrote every curse word, every filthy disgusting word I'd ever said, plus some I'd heard and never used, and some I seemed to be making up on the spot. I wrote Tyro's name again and again, so no one would imagine that this was an accident, or that I'd picked the car at random, or that this had been done by one of those ecoterrorists who burn down housing developments and chain themselves to redwoods and attack monster gas-guzzling-pig SUVs. I knew why I was doing this: because of what Tyro had done to me since I'd started at Bullywell, and mostly because of the text message he'd just sent me, supposedly from Dad. Because he'd taken what had happened to my father and turned it into a sick, cruel joke. I was doing this— trying to make him sad and miserable—because of how sad and miserable he'd made *me* feel.

Thinking about my dad suggested the finishing touch, the final flourish. I started to write "Tyro" one last time, and then I stopped after the first T and wrote "Terrorist" instead. I wrote "Tyro the Terrorist," and then I wrote it again.

The more I wrote it, the more brilliant it seemed. Tyro wanted me to feel frightened, just like the guys who'd flown into the towers had wanted us to walk around in terror. The size and scale of the damage and loss didn't seem to matter so much as the reason they did it: to hurt people, to send a message, to spread fear—just because they could.

It was cold outside, but the temperature didn't bother me. The steam my breath was making seemed to be rising from the car, like some ghostly smoke that was part of the magic trick I was doing. It looked so good, I was so proud, it was such a statement. I stepped back to admire my work. It was excellent, but it wasn't genius, it wasn't enough. I still had that boiling feeling inside me.

I bent down and picked up a chunk of cement that had come loose from the pavement. I raised it over my head and threw it through Tyro's windshield. It was a beautiful sight to see, how the window didn't exactly shatter, and it was beautiful to watch, how slowly it all happened. The glass looked as if it was melting, softening, then sinking in. The cement block disappeared, and in its place appeared a jagged hole surrounded by a huge, fantastic cobweb.

I stepped back again, thrilled with my work. I was about to call it a day and head back into school.

Just then, I felt a hand on my shoulder. I turned and saw the sweating face of Dr. Bratwurst, a few inches from mine. Behind him stood the secret-service hall monitors awaiting his orders to cuff me and throw me into a dungeon in the bowels of Bullywell, from which I would never emerge to see the light of day again.

I didn't care that they'd caught me. Let them do whatever they wanted. I was proud I'd trashed Tyro's car. I'd fought back. I'd done something. I'd gotten revenge for the crimes that Tyro and his fellow terrorists had committed.

CHAPTER NINE

NEEDLESS TO SAY, I didn't get thrown into a dungeon. I was sent home early from school. I got my own private bus ride, and—I couldn't believe my good luck!—I was given the next day off. I would have been totally happy, except that I knew: This time there wasn't a chance that I would be able to keep Mom out of the loop.

Dr. Bratwurst called that night and arranged a conference for the next morning. The meeting would include me and Mom, Tyro, his parents, and whoever else wanted to get in on the action.

For all I cared, they could sell tickets. Invite the entire school. I was pretty sure I was out of Bullywell. Bullywell and I were so completely *over*. If I was sorry at all, which I mostly wasn't, it was only because of what this might mean to Mom.

I thought I should tell her the whole truth before she had to hear it in Bratwurst's office. So that night, before dinner, we sat down in the living room, and, as calmly as I could, I told her *everything*. The ketchup, the isolation, the phone calls, every "accidental" little push and shove, and of course the locker incident. And finally the text message, and how it had sent me over the edge.

I'd been wondering how angry Mom would be about Tyro's Escalade. Because by the time I'd calmed down some, what I'd done seemed—even to me—pretty bad. But when I told her the story, all she kept saying was, "Why didn't you tell me? Sweetheart, why didn't you tell me? Why didn't I *see* this?" And then she cried, which was the worst part. "How could I not have known?" she said.

"What was I thinking, sending you to that place?"

"It's not *your* fault," I said. "You wanted me to go to a good school. You didn't know how bad it was because I didn't tell you. Plus, if you want to get technical, I lied. I kept saying everything was fine."

"Why didn't you *tell* me?" Mom said.

I didn't know how to begin to explain. All I could say was, "I don't know. I didn't want you to be unhappy. I kept thinking things would get better. I kept hoping the bullying stuff would stop by itself."

My mom cried a little more, then snuffled and wiped her tears. And I knew that she was okay when she said, "If they give us any trouble about their damn Escalade, we'll hire a lawyer. We'll sue them. We'll tell all the newspapers. Let's see what happens when people find out about that text message he sent you."

Then Mom went into the kitchen and cooked the best pot roast she'd ever made. And only later did I think how totally Mom-like it was of her not to say what I already knew perfectly well and didn't need her to say: that trashing somebody's sixty-thousand-dollar car was not exactly the smartest, most mature, most sensible way to deal with the adjustment problems I'd been having at school. She knew that. I knew that. She knew that I knew that. That lesson was already learned. The only thing left was to find out what the consequences would be and what it was going to cost us.

Mom took the Friday of the meeting off from work, so at least I didn't have to ride the loser-day-student bus, which was an instant improvement. Everything was better. Mom was with me. We breezed up the stairs and into school. I'd never been happier to walk into Bullywell. In my joy at having Mom there, at feeling protected and safe, and at finally having the truth come out, I'd practically forgotten that the reason for this meeting was my having messed up a kid's top-of-the-line, practically brand-new Cadillac.

Dr. Bratwurst came out of his office and shook Mom's hand and welcomed her to the school and mumbled something about how sorry he was to have to see her again under such unfortunate circumstances. I'd always loved Mom, obviously, but I'd never loved her quite so much as when she tore right into Dr. Bratwurst without giving him the chance to say one more word.

"You knew about this," she said. "You must have known what was happening to my son. I gather that after the locker incident you knew *all* about it. And you chose not to call me, not to inform me that my son was in physical danger, that he was being psychologically and physically abused and threatened—"

"Well, at that point it was Bart's choice," said Dr. Bratwurst. "He persuaded us not to bother you."

"And you let a thirteen-year-old make a choice like that?" demanded Mom. "And later, when the horror of his father's death was used to make him suffer, was that my son's choice, too?"

"What do you mean?" said Dr. Bratwurst.

"Someone sent him a text message and pretended to be his dead father. Someone made a vicious joke about his dad's death. Someone—"

Dr. Bratwurst actually put his hands over his ears, like a kid. Then he took them down and said, "I didn't know about that. I mean about the last part. I'd thought this whole . . . unfortunate situation ended with the locker incident. I thought it was a one-time thing. I had no idea that our students could be so heartless. I'm really and truly sorry."

I'd wrecked Tyro Bergen's fancy car, and Mom had Dr. Bratwurst apologizing! I found this so surprising and cool that I had to fight the impulse to slap Mom a giant high five. But that was when I looked past Dr. Bratwurst into his office and remembered that Mom and I weren't the only ones involved in this so-called unfortunate situation. There was Tyro, between two adults I assumed were his parents, all of them sitting on the edges of their chairs, watching us through the open door and looking none too pleased.

Tyro was glaring straight at me. I guess he

imagined that his eyes were creating some kind of force field that could shut me up and keep me from telling the truth. In his dreams, I thought. No matter how long and hard he stared at me, he couldn't scare me now. Did he really think that I was going to say I'd mutilated his car because I was bored or I didn't happen to like what was being served for lunch that day? I was going to blow the whistle on him as loud as I could because I knew perfectly well that, after this morning, Bullywell and I were history and there was nothing else he could do to me. I suppose he could have found out where I lived and hunted me down. But I didn't think that would happen. It was as if Tyro were an evil king whose magic powers evaporated at the borders of Bullywell.

Tyro's mother was—surprise!—blond and perfect-looking. You'd think she would have been eyeballing me, too, but in fact she floated a watery smile in my direction. Was it because she remembered that I was the Miracle Boy who'd lost his dad and saved his mom's life and she was trying to communicate that she still felt sorry for me about that? Or did she feel sorry for me because she knew Tyro well enough to know what he could do? I wouldn't have thought that, except that from the corner of my eye I saw Tyro's mom reach out to take his hand and Tyro pull it away. His mother looked as if she'd been crying, and I wanted to tell her: Okay, I'm sorry, but come on, it's only a car. My *dad* got killed, and I only saw my mother cry a couple of times.

Tyro's father looked like an older, sleeker Tyro. He was smiling at me, too, a grin that seemed to say, *Dude, I'm rich and powerful and confident enough to smile at anyone I choose, regardless of the circumstances, and that person will just have to smile back.* In fact, I *did* find myself smiling back, though I didn't want to. So there we all were, grinning like monkeys as we got together to discuss a whole semester of vicious bullying and a fully loaded Escalade that was going to need bodywork—a repair job that would cost about the same as a year's tuition for the other miserable-victim scholarship student who was probably going to replace me.

"Before we go any further," Dr. Bratwurst said, "we need to clear the air and get everything on the table and find out exactly what we're dealing with here. So maybe we can cut to the chase and hear from Bart what made him want to do so much damage to Tyro's vehicle. The whole story, Bart. If you will."

Dr. Bratwurst knew part of it, the locker part, already. And now he'd heard about the text message. But if he wanted to hear the *whole* story, I was going to have to start at the beginning and—just as I'd done with Mom—work my way from the ketchup stunt to the fake text message from Dad. When I got to that last part, I heard Tyro's mom gasp. What was worse was that I could tell that Mom was trying not to cry. I wished that wasn't happening. I mean, I'd already told her! More than anything, I didn't want her to cry. Not then, not there. So instead of going on and on about how painful it was to get the phony message,

I said, "Well, I guess that's all."

"My God," said Tyro's mom. "That's enough."

"What about you, Tyro?" said Dr. Bratwurst. "What's your version of the story."

"I don't know," said Tyro. "We were just kidding around. Just having fun or something. I guess it kind of got out of hand. And I'm sorry. I'm really really really sorry."

One "really" would have been enough. Three was way over the top. You could tell that no one in the room believed him, not even his own mom. His dad folded his hands and was working his knuckles as if his fingers had suddenly gotten stiff. There was a long silence, which Dr. Bratwurst broke by saying:

"Part of what's so tragic about this is that it was Mr. and Mrs. Bergen, two of the most loyal and supportive members of our board, who first saw the newspaper piece about Bart. That was during the days when we were all asking ourselves, What can *we* possibly do to help? And it was the Bergens who generously provided the endowment that has enabled Bart to attend Baileywell."

"Oh, really? I didn't know that," said Mom. But she didn't seem all that interested.

"It's true," said Dr. Bratwurst.

"Thank you very much," Mom said in the general direction of the Bergens. But she didn't seem all that grateful, either.

"The Bergens had chosen to remain anonymous," said Dr. Bratwurst. "For obvious reasons."

Obvious? The reasons were lost on me. Meanwhile, I was trying to figure out what this new information—meaning, new to *me*—might have to do with the way that Tyro had treated me. Was bullying me his way of getting back at his mom and dad? Did he see me as some kind of competition? What did *he* have to complain about? Too much money? Too much power? He had everything he wanted. Good looks, friends, popularity, both parents, and, until two days ago, an awesome SUV.

Tyro's dad cleared his throat, and you could tell that he was used to having that sound silence an entire boardroom so that everyone pretty much stopped breathing and listened to what he had to say. It certainly worked on us. We turned toward him and he focused his attention on each of us in turn, moving his head like a lizard.

"It's been an experiment," he said, and smiled, though I didn't get it. Was he saying that my being at Bullywell was his personal science project? "And I'm afraid that things haven't worked out precisely as planned. So we have two choices. We could simply cut our losses and give up on the experiment—"

That would have been *my* choice, especially if what he meant by "experiment" was me. I was the lab rat, I'd always known that, and maybe we'd come to one of those moments when the kindly researcher decides that the poor creature has been tortured enough and it's time to either put it out of its misery or set it free. Wasn't Dr. Bratwurst always—always!—saying that the point of Baileywell was to teach compassion? The most compassionate thing at this point would be to kick me out, send me back to public school, and encourage Tyro to find someone else to pick on. Which would probably take Tyro about five minutes.

Meanwhile, I kept thinking: What about the Escalade? And then it hit me: The Bergens were so rich they could afford to let it go, to be generous, to pay for the bodywork and move on. Then I remembered that the *rich* part wasn't really what was so bad about Tyro.

"Or," Tyro's dad was saying, "we can be more creative and see if we can send this little experiment into another, more successful phase." I definitely didn't like the sound of that. Maybe he was about to suggest that I should board at Bullywell, and that Tyro should be my new roommate. But before I had a chance to get too worried about that, he said, "It seems to me that both my son and Bart would be excellent candidates for our new Reach Out program."

Reach out to whom? Reach out to what? Reach out to each other? As far as I was concerned, Tyro had already done more than enough reaching out to me. Of all the things I hadn't liked so far, I liked this least, and I liked it even less when Dr. Bratwurst said, "Why, that's brilliant, brilliant! 'Creative' doesn't begin to describe it."

"What's the Reach Out program?" I asked.

"It's a new initiative that Mr. Bergen"—Dr. Bratwurst nodded at Tyro's dad—"has generously agreed to fund. And it's part of our effort to make Baileywell a warmer, more compassionate place in which to teach our students to listen to their hearts as well as their minds and their . . . well, their impulses." Mom gave me a long look and raised one eyebrow, and I loved her for not bothering to hide what she'd thought of Dr. Bratwurst's tired old routine.

"The Reach Out program," he went on, "will be a way of involving our students in the larger community, of giving them a chance to help others less fortunate than themselves. To do field-work, social service work, you might say. To *help*. There are various sites we're looking at, various areas. . . . It's all still in the early planning stages."

"Tyro and Bart would be our first two volunteers," said Mr. Bergen. I wondered what *that* meant. Were they planning to send us to Ground Zero and make us hand out burgers to the firemen and cops who were digging in search of their lost brothers? I didn't think that, with my history, they'd make me do something like that. They'd find some other hell—maybe the local maximum-security prison—and make us teach basic algebra and grammar to convicted child molesters.

The whole thing seemed strange until it struck me that what Mr. Bergen had in mind was something like sending Tyro and me to some kind of rehab program. The idea, I guessed, was that helping people in worse shape than we were would make us into better people—or at least into people who didn't go around bullying other kids or trashing expensive cars.

"I'm sorry, but I'm not working with *him*," I said. Everyone turned and stared as if they'd completely forgotten me and were shocked to remember that I was there. Meanwhile, *I* was totally shocked that all they were going to do was put us in some kind of feel-good, do-good *program*. Clearly, no one had the slightest intention of making Mom pay for the damage to Tyro's car. More surprising was the fact that no one had said a word about kicking me out of school.

Maybe I should have felt relieved. But I wasn't relieved at all. I didn't want to be there. I wished I'd had the nerve to tell them what I thought of their school and their money and their programs and their compassion. But for some reason my courage failed me, maybe because I was surrounded by grown-ups who seemed to believe that going to Bullywell was the luckiest thing that could ever happen to a human being. And that their new *program* would make it even better.

So all I could do was repeat once more that, no matter what happened, I wasn't going to be part of any program that involved my working side by side with Tyro.

For a moment Tyro's dad looked disappointed, as if that had been part of his plan. But then Tyro's mom touched him on the arm, and he looked at her and smiled and nodded. It was amazing how much the Bergens communicated without having to say a word, and I thought maybe there was something else—something important in their lives—that couldn't be mentioned or talked about, and so they'd gotten very good at silent conversation.

"Brad's probably right," said Mr. Bergen.

"Bart, dear," said his wife.

"I meant Bart," said Mr. Bergen. He looked at Mom and said, "Sorry. Senior moment. You know how it is."

"Not really," said Mom. She wasn't having any of it. She forgot things all the time, but she wasn't about to join Tyro's dad in some kind of club based on how old and brain-damaged they both were.

"Anyway, they can each start in different program areas," he went on. "Tyro in the homeless shelter. And Bart in the hospital working with sick children."

"Doing what?" said Mom. "Catching pneumonia? Getting leprosy?"

Everyone laughed, too loudly. Couldn't they tell that Mom wasn't joking?

"Of course not," said Mrs. Bergen. "We would never let him be exposed to anything contagious—"

"Doing what?" Mom repeated.

"Being with kids," said Dr. Bratwurst. "Kids who are seriously ill, sometimes terminally so. We'd just want Bart to spend some time with them, to be there, to offer them companionship and support, something to distract them from the pain and the loneliness and the long hours when their relatives can't visit and there's nothing for them to do but watch TV."

We all got quiet again, thinking of how generous and heroic this sounded, I suppose. It sounded really depressing to me, but I didn't feel I could say that.

"And I swear to you, Mrs. Rangely," Mr.

Bergen continued, "on everything we hold sacred, that Bart will never be subjected to another bullying incident during all his time at Baileywell, even if I personally have to accompany him from one class to another."

"Yikes," I said. The thought was so horrifying that the word just leaped out, and everyone smiled.

"Mr. Bergen's right," said Dr. Bratwurst. "I give you my word, too. My word of honor. You *do* believe me, don't you?" Neither Mom nor I could bring ourselves to say, No, sorry, we don't, we're not interested. No second chances. But when had we become the ones who could decide whether or not to give *them* second chances? I was the one who'd trashed a car.

And that's how I got suckered into another term at Bullywell.

Christmas was pretty much like Thanksgiving, only with presents. More presents than usual, actually, more presents than ever before, because

I guess everyone was trying to make it up to me for how much I had lost. It didn't work. I missed my dad. I kept thinking that maybe he would have known what to do about Tyro and his gang.

Christmas Eve dinner at Gran's was fantastic, as usual, with course after course of all kinds of bizarre sea creatures that I used to hate as a little kid but that I loved now, especially the baked clams stuffed with bread crumbs and garlic.

But I couldn't really enjoy the dinner, and everyone noticed that I wasn't eating much. They kept hugging me and pinching my cheeks and telling me I looked pale. I knew they thought the problem was that this was my first Christmas without Dad. And it *was* a problem, especially when it was added to the problem of looking forward to another semester at Bullyville, plus the additional problem of making up for damaging Tyro's car by spending two afternoons a week with kids with oxygen masks and bald heads and tubes sticking out of their arms.

* * *

The day before school started again, Mom drove me to Jersey Memorial for an orientation session with Mrs. Straus, the hospital social worker. Mom insisted on coming with me, because she wanted to be extra sure that I wouldn't be exposed to pneumonia or cholera or bubonic plague or whatever she imagined.

Fortunately, Mrs. Straus's office was right near the hospital entrance, so—for now, at least—I didn't have to walk through corridors lined with gurneys and wheelchairs and rooms into which I could peek at some poor kid drawing his last rattling breath.

For some reason I expected someone ancient. But Mrs. Straus was young, tall, redheaded, sort of stylish: She looked like an actress who might play a tough but warmhearted district attorney on TV. She rose to shake my hand, then Mom's, and I could tell right away that she knew everything about us: about Dad, about the Miracle Boy, about the bullying at Bullywell, about what I'd done to Tyro's car, and about how I would never

179

be here if the Bergens and Dr. Bratwurst hadn't decided that I was in serious need of the good-deed, Good Samaritan equivalent of reform school. I felt I had to fight the impulse to turn to jelly and sit there and let her tell me everything I needed to know and everything I was going to have to do. So I decided to come out swinging.

"So what do I have to do?" I asked. "Put on a clown nose like that stupid doctor Robin Williams played in that crappy movie, and go around seeing if some bald kid would like me to tell stupid jokes and pull rabbits out of a hat? That is, if you let people *bring* rabbits into the hospital, which I don't think would be very sanitary. Or maybe I'm supposed to get a kazoo and get the kids to sing cheery songs about how they're feeling better and better, stronger and stronger every day. Or maybe—"

"Bart, please. Slow down," said Mrs. Straus, very gently. "This is not *Patch Adams*. No one's going to force you to do anything you don't want to do. Why don't you just calm down and relax and listen to what I'm suggesting?" I was relieved when Mrs. Straus made me stop talking and I could just sit back and listen.

"You'll come two afternoons a week," she said. "From three till five. We'll arrange to have you picked up at school."

Well, fine. That was okay with me. It meant I'd be saved from art club, where all last semester Kristin had supervised one "conceptual" project after another, so that at the end of each session we threw out everything we'd done.

"You'll be assigned from one to three of our kids," Mrs. Straus was saying. "So, no, it won't be like wandering the corridors in a clown nose. Basically, your job is just to hang out with them, keep them company, make them feel as if they haven't completely lost contact with the outside world. Many of them have been in the hospital for quite a long time, so they might want to know about all the latest things kids are into—"

"I don't always know about that," I said. I was thinking that if I'd spent months in the hospital,

I'd pretty much lose interest in the latest cartoons and which edition of Doom kids were playing now.

"It's not a test," said Mrs. Straus. "No one's going to quiz you on whether you get it right. The important thing, as I said, is to *be* with them. To be present."

I said, "Wouldn't they rather be with sick kids like themselves? Wouldn't they have more in common?"

"You might think so," said Mrs. Straus. "But it doesn't always work like that. Sometimes they want to be reminded that there's a world out there, a world that they'll reenter when they get better."

"Are they going to get better?" asked Mom.

There was silence after that. Then Mrs. Straus said, "Many of them will. We hope. That's why they're here."

"What about their families?" I said. "Don't *they* come visit?"

"Their parents work," said Mrs. Straus. "Their brothers and sisters go to school. The families are usually here on weekends and in the evenings. But we've found, from studies, that late afternoons—especially in the winter, when it gets dark early—are the loneliest and scariest times for our kids. And that's where you come in."

I wanted to say that late afternoons were not exactly my favorite time of day, either. But I knew that I didn't have a chance of winning any kind of discussion with Mrs. Social Worker District Attorney. I was healthy, I was free. These kids had no choice but to watch the sun set and the darkness gather outside their hospital-room windows. I was sorry for them, I really and truly was. But it wasn't my problem.

And then something happened. It was almost as if I was standing outside myself and watching a nicer, more compassionate version of me say, "All right. I think I can do that."

Mrs. Straus told me a few more things, such as not to ask the kids what was wrong with them, what diseases they had. I could let them talk about their illnesses if they wanted to, but I shouldn't make that the focus of our conversations. My job was to find out what they were interested in, what they cared about, what might make them feel connected to the world outside the hospital. My job, said Mrs. Straus, was to be "the breath of fresh air that blows in when we open the door."

Right, I thought. Sure. Then I saw Mom looking at me, all proud and teary-eyed. And once again, as always that year, I found myself wanting to make Mom happy, because I imagined that her happiness would filter down and sprinkle, like some kind of magic dust, on me.

CHAPTER TEN

FAT FREDDIE, THE day-student bus driver, was assigned to drive me from school to the hospital. The prospect of riding alone in the bus, just me and Fat Freddie, gave me the serious creeps. I imagined Freddie kidnapping me and throwing me into a trench he had dug in his basement and telling the world he had no idea why I hadn't shown up at the appointed spot when he'd come to pick me up at the hospital for the drive back home.

But the Fat Freddie who drove me from the

school to the hospital seemed like an entirely different person from the silent, crabby Fat Freddie who drove me and the other losers to and from school. It turned out that Fat Freddie had a nephew who'd been hit by a car that broke half the bones in his body. The nephew had gone to this very same hospital and spent six months there, and they'd completely fixed him up. Good as new, said Freddie. Now the only thing you could tell—and you really had to look hard—was that Fat Freddie's nephew had a tiny limp and one of his arms was a few inches shorter than the other. Judging from the way that Fat Freddie treated me on the way to the hospital, you would have thought that I was the surgeon who'd operated on his nephew.

Fat Freddie said I was doing God's work, and when I got off the bus at the hospital, he said, "God bless you, son. See you right here in a couple of hours. Don't worry if there's traffic and I'm a few minutes late. Don't worry, I'll be right here, trust me."

That seemed like a good sign, as did the fact that I found Mrs. Straus's office without getting lost and having to ask and be interrogated by the hospital security guards. This time, Mrs. Straus gave me a quick hug, as if we were old friends.

As we left her office, Mrs. Straus put her arm around my shoulder, which was sort of nice and at the same time sort of worrisome, as if she thought I might need encouragement and support for what was coming next. This time, I knew, I wasn't going to be spared the gurneys and the wheelchairs and the corridors lined with sick kids.

I was glad that Mom wasn't with me, because I didn't want her to worry about what diseases I might catch. The doctors who passed us seemed to be in a hurry, or to have something serious on their minds, but every so often a nurse would smile at us in a way that reminded me of the gooey way people smiled at me when I was still the Miracle Boy who'd saved his mother. Whether I was here as a patient or a visitor or as punishment for trashing a kid's SUV didn't seem to matter.

The mere presence of a kid in the hospital was reason enough for people to flash me that silly smile.

We went up in an elevator that stopped on every floor. Doctors and nurses got on and off, along with visitors. The minute I looked at each visitor, I could more or less tell how sick the patient was whom that person was going to see. The happy ones got off at the maternity floor. Several carried shiny pink or blue smiley-face balloons. I imagined them standing at the glass windows through which they could see the newborn babies, holding the balloons. The grim passengers and the ones who seemed to have been crying got off at the higher floors, where people were, I imagined, recovering from surgery or suffering from illnesses from which they were probably not going to get better.

Right from the start, I felt close to these people. I wanted to tell them that I knew what it was like, what it was like to be *really* scared and feel lost and have someone you love die. At the same time, I wanted to get as far away from them as possible. A couple of women—moms, I guessed—got off at the pediatric floor with me and Mrs. Straus. We pushed our way through a swinging door, and then I had to stop for a minute, because I felt a little dizzy, on the edge of being sick. Maybe it was the smell: disinfectant and soap and something sweet—to tell the truth, a little like baby shit— that I couldn't identify, and didn't want to.

"Are you all right?" asked Mrs. Straus.

"I'm fine," I said. "It must have been something I ate for lunch—"

Without a word, Mrs. Straus led me into a kind of waiting room, which was empty except for some chairs and a soda machine. She bought me a soda, and for a few minutes we sat in silence while I sipped from the can.

"Feeling better?" she asked.

"Sure," I said. "I'm okay."

So off we went, down a corridor, and it was just as I'd pictured it. Maybe a little worse. Mostly I kept my eyes straight ahead, trying not to look on either side, but every so often I couldn't help it and I let myself peek. Sure enough, there was some tiny head peering out from under the covers, or a bald kid staring at a TV blaring from a corner near the ceiling.

Outside each door was the kind of whiteboard you could wipe clean, and on each board was a kid's first name written in colored marker and decorated with flowers and balloons and more smiley faces. Without knowing where you were, you could tell—just from looking at the art—that you were in a doctor's office or hospital, somewhere kids were sick, and where some fool imagined that a pack of bright markers and a drawing of a daisy or a clown was just what they needed to cheer them up. The signs were probably helpful for the nurses and the doctors who could never remember patients' names. They could check outside the door and go sailing into the room, full of confidence, singing out, "Hi, Jimmy . . . Hi, Johnny . . . Hi, Jane."

In my case, it was going to be Hi, Ramón.

That was the first room we stopped outside, and I could tell from the rubbed-off, smeary look of the whiteboard that Ramón hadn't exactly gotten there yesterday.

"Let's visit Ramón," said Mrs. Straus cheerily, as if she thought this was *fun*, as if she'd somehow forgotten that this was my punishment assignment. She was acting as if this were a friendly "visit" I'd decided to make on my own.

In the bed a tiny kid with the covers pulled up to his neck was lying with his eyes closed. It was clear, at least to me, that Ramón was asleep or pretending to be asleep. He obviously didn't want visitors, or if he did want one, I wasn't the visitor he wanted.

"Ramón," said Mrs. Straus, "this is Bart. He's come to hang out with you for a while."

Ramón's eyes blinked open. Then he closed them again. Ramón's joy at seeing me left me and Mrs. Straus pretty much stranded. What was our next move supposed to be?

"Well," said Mrs. Straus brightly. "Why don't I

leave Bart here for a few minutes so you two can get acquainted? Maybe you guys will have an easier time of it if I'm not here cramping your style."

I stared at her, goggle-eyed. I must have looked panicky, because she held up both hands, fingers splayed. I understood. Ten minutes.

I pulled the armchair up to Ramón's bedside.

"So, Ramón," I said. "What's up? How's it going?"

No answer.

"How long have you been here?" I said.

Nothing.

"Where do you live?"

Silence.

"So, like, have you got any brothers and sisters?"

Not a word.

"You like to play sports or anything like that?" Even as it popped out, I knew that it was a completely idiotic question. And Ramón seemed to know it, too, because he rolled away from me and turned his face to the wall.

Mrs. Straus had said that the only important thing was being here. Being with them. And she'd said this wasn't a test. I was just paying for some damage I'd done to a bully's SUV. It didn't matter if Ramón liked me or not, or wanted me to be here or not, or whether I felt totally ridiculous or not. All that counted was that I put in my time, and then we could call it quits. Everyone could go home happy. Or anyway, *I* could.

So I just sat there, watching the minutes pass. Who knows what Ramón was thinking. He probably just wanted me to go away. It seemed to me that Ramón needed some kind of help beyond whatever the doctors were giving him. Ramón needed a lot more than a visit from me. But most likely they knew that. No one could really believe that I was just the ticket to bring Ramón out of his depression or stupor or coma or whatever.

After what seemed like a dozen years, Mrs. Straus reappeared. I was never happier to see anyone in my life.

"Did you guys have a good visit?" she said.

I said, "I don't think Ramón felt like talking all that much."

"Well, maybe next time," said Mrs. Straus. "Bye for now, Ramón."

"Bye," I said.

We waited for Ramón to say good-bye. He didn't.

When we were out in the hall, I said, "He didn't say a word. *Can* he talk?"

"Of course he can talk," said Mrs. Straus. "And he will. Ramón's just going through a bit of a rough spot. Maybe when he gets more used to you."

When would that be? I wondered. I thought of Tyro dishing out disgusting cafeteria food to lines of homeless men. I almost wished we'd drawn each other's job. The homeless guys would at least say thank you and not leave me, as Ramón had just done, feeling useless and lame and embarrassed.

"Don't worry," said Mrs. Straus. "Ramón will warm up to you. Meanwhile, let's go see Stimmer.

Trust me. Meeting Stimmer will be very different from your visit with Ramón."

I would have gone anywhere if someone promised me that it would be different from Ramón's room. But Mrs. Straus was smiling in a way that made me think I might not like my time with Stimmer, whoever *that* was, any better than my "visit" with Ramón.

Stimmer, it seemed, was an artist. He'd colored his own whiteboard, so that his name was done graffiti style, in cartoony letters, like something you'd see, as you rode on a train, up on a rooftop or a ledge or in the center of a tunnel, and you couldn't imagine how anyone had been brave or stupid or crazy enough to want to sign his name there.

To go along with the whole artist thing, Stimmer had convinced the nurses to let him wear his street clothes, which, in Stimmer's case, meant a fluffy cap with a bill, a tight maroon jacket, checked pants, and big aviator sunglasses. Stimmer lay on top of the covers, his long, lean body bent slightly to fit the too-small bed. Even as I was thinking that Stimmer must have been pushing the top age limit of the children's floor, it struck me that he was the first black kid I'd met since I left public school. There wasn't one—not one—in the whole Bullywell population.

Probably Dr. Bratwurst had tried his hardest to get a black kid to go there, but I guessed he couldn't find any parents willing to subject their kid to being the only black student in an entire school. And considering how they'd tortured *me*, I couldn't even begin to imagine how the Bullywell bullies would treat someone who belonged to a racial minority.

Stimmer glanced up at me, but he was way too cool to change his expression from a look of boredom.

"Stimmer, this is Bart," said Mrs. Straus. "He's part of a new program—"

"Oh, I get it," said Stimmer. "Buy the sick kid a paid friend. Or maybe we didn't buy him, maybe he's just rented for the day."

"I wouldn't say that," said Mrs. Straus. "I wouldn't say that at all."

But *I* would have said it. That's *exactly* what I would have said if I'd thought of it. I looked at Stimmer and practically burst out laughing. Right from the start, it was as if it was the two of us against Mrs. Straus, who'd done nothing to deserve the smirks we were giving her.

"Whatever," said Stimmer. "Come on in. You might as well earn whatever they're paying you. How much they paying you, anyhow? Maybe it might be more fair if we split it down the middle."

"They're not paying me anything, actually." I hated how nervous and stiff I sounded.

Stimmer looked at me as if I was the biggest fool he'd ever met.

"Come on," he said. "Don't tell me you doing this for *free*. Are you trying to do some kind of good deed?"

"Well, then," interrupted Mrs. Straus. "I can see that you two are getting along famously. So I'll just make myself scarce and come back in a while and pick Bart up."

"Make it quick," said Stimmer, which, I thought, didn't bode all that well for the great new friendship that Mrs. Straus seemed to think was developing. But she'd already left, and didn't hear him.

"So come on," said Stimmer as I pulled the chair up next to his bed. "How much *are* they paying you? What are you doing the Florence Nightingale thing for?"

I could see there was no point lying to Stimmer. I could tell he'd get the truth out of me sooner or later.

"Actually," I said, "it's sort of a community service thing."

"You volunteered to hang out here? What are you? Stupid?"

"I didn't exactly volunteer," I said.

Stimmer considered this for a few seconds and then said, "So, what happened? You get busted? Buying a joint from an undercover cop hanging out near the schoolyard, something like that?"

"No," I said. And then, just because I felt like saying it, and because I wanted to hear how it sounded, and because something about being with Stimmer made me suddenly feel almost proud of it, I said, "This kid was giving me a hard time in school. I got even. I trashed his SUV. Scratched the paint job, busted the windshield. So now I'm kind of like, you know, making amends."

"No shit," said Stimmer. "That *is* cool. That's way cooler than I imagined. You don't look like the kind of guy who'd do something like that."

"Thanks," I said. I couldn't help feeling pleased even though I wasn't sure it was meant as a compliment.

"What kind of ride was it?" asked Stimmer.

"Cadillac Escalade," I said. "White. Top of the line."

Stimmer whistled through his teeth, long and low. "That is *excellent*. So this is like punishment detail, right? Hang with the sick kids for a while, and they agree not to nail you for messing with some rich kid's vehicle?"

"Sort of. I guess you could say that."

"Right," said Stimmer. "I get it now. The picture becomes clear." And he instantly lost interest. We sat in silence for a while, watching TV. On the screen, a white guy in a stocking cap was showing off his fancy house: game room, pool table, pinball machine, humongous flat-screen TV.

"Nice crib," said Stimmer. "Not bad at all."

"I'd take it," I said.

"Sweet," said Stimmer. "Except that you don't see the guy actually turn on the TV or work the pinball machine. Ever notice that? Because these dudes are always too dumb to know *how* to turn on the TV and make the machine run. That's why he's got to have an entourage, probably a butler and a maid."

In a high voice, he said, "Jeeves, my good man, could you please get your white ass over here and turn on the television set?"

Okay. This was more like it. This felt like something you might do with an actual friend, watch TV and insult the people on it. I wondered why Stimmer was in the hospital. He seemed healthy, energetic enough. Actually, he seemed overly energetic, bouncing on his bed and snorting each time the white guy with the fancy house said something stupid.

Then abruptly Stimmer switched off the TV and turned to face me.

"I've got an idea," he said. "I mean if you're really my friend, my new best friend, why don't you *act* like a friend?"

"Like do . . . what?" Here it comes, I thought.

"Why don't you give me a part of your liver?" Stimmer said. "Just a teensy piece. A baby bite. It'll grow back on its own. That's what I'm doing in here, waiting for a liver transplant. I'm probably at the bottom of the list, down below anybody who happens to be related to a big CEO or a movie star or somebody in the government. And I'm probably going to die if I don't get a chunk of somebody's liver. So why not *you*, dog? Isn't that what friends do for friends?"

"Gosh," I said. "I don't know. I don't know if I could do that." I felt like a coward or a completely selfish person. But I didn't want to have surgery and give up part of my liver for someone I'd just met. I mean, I would have done it for Mom or Gran if they needed it, maybe even my aunts or cousins. But I'd only walked into Stimmer's room five minutes ago. On the other hand, no one in my family needed a liver—no one that I knew about—and Stimmer did. It seemed like a pretty high price to pay for taking my house keys to Tyro's Escalade. Still, it was the right thing to do.

By now I was so confused that I couldn't speak. Stimmer took one look at me and read the answer in my face.

"Is that a negative?" he said.

"Yes," I said. "I mean no. I can't. I'm sorry."

"Not *can't*. You mean you *won't*. Some friend." He turned away from me and looked up at the TV.

And that was how we were—not talking, watching TV—when Mrs. Straus came back to get me.

"How did you two get along?" she asked.

"Great," said Stimmer. "Slammin'. Just don't bring the dude back again, okay?"

"But Stimmer—"

"Don't mess with me, okay?" he said. "You pull any of this funny shit again, I'm complaining to the doctor and the nurses. I've got some rights here, too."

Mrs. Straus looked at me, and I rocketed out of my chair.

"Bye," I said, but Stimmer didn't reply.

"What happened?" asked Mrs. Straus when we were out in the hall.

"Things were going fine. And then he asked me to give him part of my liver."

"Oh, the poor kid," said Mrs. Straus, and tears sprang to her eyes. "He asks everyone. I should have anticipated that. I should have warned you."

"I guess you can't blame him," I said.

Mrs. Straus shot me a quick look. "What did you tell him?"

"I told him I was sorry." I couldn't look at her.

"*I'm* sorry," she said. "I should have seen it coming. Don't feel guilty, Bart. He shouldn't have asked you. I shouldn't have let it happen."

"That's okay," I said. "It's not your fault." It was strange that I was the one trying to make Mrs. Straus feel better about my second strikeout in a row. She'd said I'd only have to meet three kids today, which was reassuring. I only had one more spectacular failure and humiliation to go, and then I was free to leave and find Fat Freddie and take my pitiful self home.

"Don't despair." How did Mrs. Straus know that was what I'd been doing? "I've saved the best for last. You'll love Nola, everyone does. The nurses fight to take care of her. She's a total trip. And I just know that Nola will love you back."

It was just occurring to me that Nola was a girl, and that—if you didn't count my girl cousins, which I didn't—I hadn't even *talked* to a girl since I left public school. I was afraid that I might have forgotten *how* to talk to a girl, not that I ever knew, exactly.

For a moment I let myself imagine that Nola was an incredibly beautiful hot chick suffering from some not-so-bad disease of which she was just about to be cured, at which point she would leave the hospital and become my girlfriend. Then I thought: With my luck, she'll be the bald one or the burn victim or the one with the hideous skin condition that wasn't catching but you still didn't want to look at it. Well, fine. I would visit my three sick kids, make my quota. I'd get through my first day of reaching out, and then I would be free to go home no matter how badly I'd done.

Walking into Nola's room, I practically had to fight my way past a small army of teddy bears and stuffed animals. Many of them still had gift cards and get-well-soon messages tied around their furry necks. Obviously Nola was extremely popular.

I saw the face of a little girl staring at me from among all the stuffed-animal faces. She was maybe nine or ten, and I guess she would have been really cute except that her face was a brilliant, glow-in-the-dark shade of yellow.

"Nola, this is Bart," said Mrs. Straus. "He's come to hang out with you."

Nola narrowed her eyes and stared at me. You could tell she was smart, just by looking at her. She didn't say anything; she only raised one eyebrow.

"Hi, Nola!" I said, too loud, like a total jerk.

"Hello." Nola was one of those little kids with a weirdly deep, throaty, smoker's voice.

I remembered Mrs. Straus telling me not to ask what condition the kids had, not to make a deal about their diseases, not to do anything that would make them feel worse about being sick. But the color of Nola's skin—that blazing canary yellow—was so intense that I couldn't stop myself from staring.

Nola and I looked at each other. Once more, I dimly heard Mrs. Straus tell us what fun we were going to have between now and whenever she was coming to get me.

There was a long silence. Then Nola said, "It's chameleonitis. In case you're wondering. That's my diagnosis, that's what I've got."

"Excuse me?"

"You should see me in the blue room," she said. "I turn this totally crazy cobalt color."

I couldn't believe how slow I was! Because only now did I look around and see that the walls were the same yellow, more or less, as Nola's skin, which was part of what made the whole thing seem so peculiar.

I said, "You're kidding. That *is* a joke, right?"

"Ask my doctors if you don't believe me," she said. And she raised that one eyebrow again and looked as if she was trying to figure out exactly how retarded I was.

I had no idea where I got the nerve to say, "You know, you're kind of bratty for a little kid."

"Self-defense," she said. "You wouldn't believe what having people stick you with needles all day long does for your personality."

"Have you been in here a long time?" I asked.

"Since I was born," she said.

I said, "You're kidding about that, too, right?"

I wanted her to be joking.

"I've been in here a lot. On and off. They keep saying they know how to fix what's wrong with me, and then it turns out they *don't* know how to fix it, and *then* it turns out they don't even know what's wrong with me."

I kept wanting to ask what they *thought* it was, what had turned her that color.

"How old are you?" I said instead.

"Ten," said Nola.

I thought how strange it was to meet a ten-year-old who sort of reminded me of my mom.

It seemed like we'd run out of things to say when Nola asked, "So what are you doing here? Are you one of those kids who get off on hanging with sick and wounded freaks?"

"No," I said. "Of course not, no way. I—"

"Don't feel bad if you are. I don't care. To tell you the truth, I'm glad for some company. I don't care who it is."

"Thanks a lot," I said.

"Sorry," said Nola. "I didn't mean that the way

it sounds. It just gets so boring here watching soap operas all day on TV. I don't know why you can't get the cartoon channel in this place, but you can't. The hospital's too cheap, I guess."

"Doesn't your family visit you?" I couldn't believe I was asking Nola such a personal question, I'd only just met her.

"Sure, pretty much every evening and all weekend. But my parents work all day, my brother and sister go to school, so I'm mostly on my own till the evening visiting hours. And as you may have noticed, the other kids on the ward are not exactly a barrel of laughs."

"I noticed," I said.

"I keep hoping someone fun will show up, but no one ever does."

"That'll be me," I said. "Mr. Fun."

"Right," said Nola. "So what *are* you doing here?"

I wanted to tell her the truth, because it seemed like the right thing to do but also because something about Nola's clear blue eyes, shining out of that strange yellow face, made you think that she could see right through you and that she would know if you were lying. On the other hand, I didn't want to tell her about trashing Tyro's car. I wanted her to think well of me, or anyway, not to think I was the kind of person who'd solve a problem that way.

I said, "It's a kind of community service thing. You know, like when celebrities get busted for something and they wind up getting their picture taken with some poor kid on their lap and a book propped open. Well, it's kind of like that."

"Did you get busted?" said Nola, perking up. "For what? Shoplifting? Drugs?"

I said, "I got into trouble at school—"

"What kind of trouble?"

"I don't feel like talking about it."

"That's okay," Nola said. "I can respect that. So your school made you come here to punish you for what you did?"

"You got it," I said. "Not that it's punishment—"

210

"And you're supposed to be my babysitter or guardian angel or something?"

"Not exactly." I could feel myself blushing. "More just like somebody to hang out with."

"What school do you go to?" she asked.

"Bullywell," I said. "I mean, Baileywell."

"Poor you!" Nola rolled her eyes.

"So you know about it?"

"Doesn't everybody?" she said. "Doesn't everybody know about Alcatraz? Sing Sing? San Quentin? Devil's Island?"

I thought: She sure knows a lot of prison names for a ten-year-old kid. And then I thought: Her whole life must be like a jail.

"So where do you live?" said Nola.

"Hillbrook." I made a face.

"What does your dad do?" she asked.

"Did," I said. "He worked in the World Trade Center. He was killed on 9/11."

Tears popped into Nola's eyes. "Holy smokes," she said, then clapped her hand over her mouth. "Oh, I'm so sorry. I'm such a creep. I'm an idiot. I didn't mean to say that."

"That's okay," I said.

"Your *dad*," she said. "That's the worst thing I ever heard."

It was odd. I did and didn't want Nola to feel sorry for me. "It happened to a lot of people," I said stupidly. "A lot of kids' dads."

"I know that," she said. "But it was *your* dad."

I said, "He'd left us, anyway."

"What?" said Nola.

"Six months before he died. He left me and Mom to go live with this slut who worked in his office."

"That's even worse," said Nola.

"What do you mean?" I said, though I sort of knew. In fact, it was what *I* thought. But I'd never heard anyone else say it. Maybe the reason no one had ever said that was that I'd never told anyone. It was this awful secret me and Mom had, and I'd never trusted anyone enough to let them in on it. So that made it even stranger—I mean, that I had just let it slip out the very first time I met this blue-eyed, yellow-faced little girl propped up in her hospital bed.

"What about your mom?" said Nola.

"She worked there, too," I said.

"No," said Nola. "Oh, no. Please tell me you're not like a total orphan."

"I'm not," I said. "My mom was supposed to go to work that morning. But I had the flu, I was home sick from school, and she stayed home with me, and it saved her life. There were stories about it in all the papers. I was really famous for about fifteen minutes. I was the Miracle Boy. I kept expecting people to ask me to pray for them and stuff."

A funny expression passed over Nola's face. "Wait a minute," she said. "I heard about that somewhere. Maybe I even read about you. I don't know. It's like I already *know* that story."

"Everybody knew that story," I said. "And now I'm ready for everybody to forget it. It just makes the whole thing about my dad a million times more complicated."

"I've already forgotten," Nola said. "I've forgotten the whole thing. You're secret's safe with me."

"What secret?" someone said, and we both turned to see Mrs. Straus standing in the doorway, beaming. "Why, that's fantastic!" she said. "Already you two have a secret."

"When are you coming back?" Nola asked me.

"Friday," I said. I checked with Mrs. Straus. Suddenly I was afraid that, after my failures with Ramón and Stimmer, they weren't going to let me come back at all. Maybe I'd be transferred to the homeless shelter to work with Tyro. And then it struck me that the time I'd spent talking to Nola was the longest I'd gone without thinking about Tyro since I'd started at Bullywell. What was even more bizarre was that Tyro no longer seemed so scary. Though I never would have said this to anyone, it felt almost as if Nola was *my* guardian angel, keeping me safe.

"You know what?" Mrs. Straus said as I was leaving. "Since it worked out so well with Nola, why don't we leave Ramón and Stimmer for some other time? Some other volunteer. Maybe as the program expands we'll find someone more in sync with their needs. You can just come visit Nola."

For a moment I felt guilty for not being more in sync, whatever that was. But I let it go, because the last thing I wanted was for Mrs. Straus to decide that maybe I *should* hang out with Ramón and Stimmer until we *did* get more in sync.

"That's fine with me," I said, and it was.

When I got to the front of the hospital, Fat Freddie was waiting for me in the bus.

"How did you do with the kids?" he said.

"I killed it," I said. "I really did. I was everybody's new best friend. And you know what? One little girl called me her guardian angel."

"Bless your heart," Fat Freddie said.

"Thank you, Frederick," I said.

CHAPTER ELEVEN

THE MINUTE I WALKED into school after Christmas vacation, I could feel the change, like a shift in the weather or a sudden rise in the barometric pressure. I was no longer one of the bullied, no longer a victim.

Maybe it was just because the second semester had begun, and I'd survived the first term. Maybe it was because three new kids had enrolled at Bullywell for the second term, and the bullies had fresh meat to pick over. Or maybe Tyro's parents had leaned on him to call off his team of thugs. I didn't care *why* it happened, but I liked the result. The bullying—I mean the bullying of *me*—had stopped just as suddenly as it had started.

No one called me Fart Strangely, no one tripped me or pushed me, no one sent me hate text messages. No one drowned my lunch in condiments. And somehow I knew that they weren't going to. Without the daily torture to worry about, I could actually pay attention to my classes. They weren't difficult, they weren't easy. It was school. I was fine.

I figured I could stick it out until June and then I'd bring the subject up again with Mom. Over the summer I'd persuade her that, scholarship or no scholarship, it was time for me to go back to public school. Bullywell wasn't the place for me. I promised myself that by next year I'd be back in my old school, and I'd have my old friends back, and my life would return to something as close to normal as it would ever be again.

When Mom asked, I told her that the bullying had stopped. She knew I was telling her the truth this time, and I could tell she was relieved. She stopped asking me if I'd made any friends, so I no longer had to lie about that. Okay, I didn't have any friends at school, but I no longer had any enemies, and for now that was good enough.

Besides, I had Nola. Every Wednesday and Friday, I went to visit her. We always found things to talk about, and it was amazing, because she never went anywhere or did anything, but she always had something interesting to say. For example, she'd tell me her dreams, and while it's usually really boring to listen to other people's dreams, hers were always fascinating and strange. Once she told me that she dreamed she was getting married to a giant squid, and she was in a bridal dress and the squid was in a top hat and tails. Another day she told me she dreamed she was on a cloud with a lion and a tiger and a gorilla, and the animals kept spitting on people who were walking around down on the earth. She read a lot, and she told me the plots of books that, I noticed, often involved people who had been shrunk to the size of tiny insects or else magnified into giants. We always laughed at the same things. We laughed till tears came into our eyes, though often I couldn't have said exactly what was so funny.

When it was time to leave, I always asked her if there was anything she wanted me to bring her the next time I came. At first she said no, no thanks. Maybe she was afraid that if she asked for anything, I'd stop coming back. But after a while, she must have trusted me more, because she'd make little requests, nothing complicated or hard to find. And on the weekends, when I'd go shopping with my mom, I'd try to get what she wanted. Sometimes it was food, like a tangerine or strawberries. Sometimes it was a book she wanted and couldn't get from the rolling cart they brought around the wards.

Mom was always glad to help me get what Nola wanted. She liked hearing about Nola. She said, *"That's* what's going to teach you about compassion. Not whatever that dopey Dr. Bratton—"

"Dr. Bratwurst," I said.

It took Mom a minute to get it. Then she laughed.

"I mean, Dr. Bratwurst," she said.

One day, when I asked Nola if there was anything she wanted me to bring her, she said, "Actually, yes. But it's not something you can bring, exactly. It's just something I really want, something you can help me do."

"What's that?" I asked.

"I'd like to get out of here," Nola said. "I'd like you to help me escape."

"Er . . . how we would do *that*?" I asked.

"Lots of ways," she said. "You could bring me some clothes, like maybe *your* clothes, and I could dress up like a normal person and just walk out of here. Or else we could do something dramatic, like pull the fire alarm, and then when everyone was running around evacuating the place, I could slip out."

"I think that one's illegal," I said. "Pulling the fire alarm."

"Okay," said Nola. "Back to Plan A."

After that we used to talk about it. We'd plan what I was going to bring her, what she was going to wear. I could never tell how serious Nola was. I kept thinking that I'd also have to bring some of my mom's makeup, because no matter what Nola wore, someone was bound to notice that we were trying to smuggle a bright yellow person out of the hospital. Also I'd wonder what we were supposed to do with all the tubes and bottles she was attached to, and beyond that, what I would do with *her*, where I would bring her. Home to live with me and Mom? Not even Mom would go for that. To say nothing of the fact that, whether I liked to admit it or not, Nola was sick. What would I do if she got worse? Mainly, the whole subject made me realize how brave Nola was, and how strong. She never felt sorry for herself or gave up, and she never wanted anyone to feel sorry for her.

From time to time I would forget that she was sick. And then one afternoon I would get to her room and she would be lying there with her eyes closed, and I would say, "Nola, how are you feeling?"

"I'm excellent," she'd say. "I couldn't be more excellent."

Still, I could tell she was making an effort to open her eyes and look as if she was all right. By the time I left, I could also tell that she was sort of glad I was going, because she was tired and not feeling well, and she needed to rest.

Pretty soon, I couldn't help noticing that I was thinking about Nola even when I wasn't with her. It was almost as if I had a crush on her. How weird was that? Having a crush on a little kid with some kind of mysterious disease. But it wasn't as if I wanted to date her or ask her to a dance or make out with her or anything. It was more like I had a crush on her *spirit*. I felt like she knew what I was thinking without my having to say it. I felt like she *got* me—all the best things about me. And I felt like all the good things about *her* rubbed off on me when I was with her.

Being around Nola made me feel smarter and

funnier and nicer. And having her as a friend made me feel better about what had happened to me, about losing my dad, and the towers falling, and life in general. She was the only high spot in my life that year.

It was embarrassing, but whenever Fat Freddie dropped me off at the hospital—as soon as he pulled away from the curb—I always began to speed walk, and then to run. I was that eager to see Nola. I couldn't run *in* the hospital, of course, but I was still moving fast.

Sometimes, not very often, Nola talked about being sick. Once she told me how, when she was five, she'd slipped into a coma, and that had been the first real sign that something was seriously wrong. She'd been in kindergarten, and they'd been playing some stupid game like Simon Says, and suddenly she started feeling like she was at the bottom of an aquarium.

"Underwater?" I said. "As in *drowning*?"

"Sort of," said Nola. "But more like I was swimming, like I was a fish surrounded by other fish. All the other kids turned into minnows and angelfish and striped tropical fish, and the mean ones were nasty fish, baby sharks and piranhas, and they were all swimming past me. I could see their bright, beady fish eyes and watch their gills pumping. And my teacher was the biggest fish, almost like a whale, she just kept getting bigger and bigger. Her voice was booming, and the last thing I remember hearing before I passed out was her superloud, echoey voice saying, 'Nola, pay attention!' Then, 'Nola, are you okay?'"

"Were you?" I asked. "You *were* okay, right?"

"Eventually," said Nola. "But first I died."

"You *what*?"

"I died," Nola said. "I was clinically dead. And you know what? It's true, or *sort of* true, what people say about seeing this light-filled tunnel. Except that they always make it sound like some heavenly tunnel, and I kept thinking I was in an *actual* tunnel. I mean, like the Holland Tunnel. I thought we were driving into the city, and the lights were splashing all over the ceiling like they do on rainy days."

"Then what?"

"They brought me back," she said. "The doctors saved me. I don't know how. I wasn't supposed to know I'd been dead, but I read it in my chart. None of the doctors or nurses knew I could read yet, so they would just leave my records lying around, and I read them. That's how I found out that I'd died."

"Wow" was all I could say.

I got up and went over to the window. Tears had filled my eyes, and I didn't want Nola to see. Because it seemed to me that if she'd died once, she might die again, and I didn't want *that* to happen. It made me think of the other dead person I knew—namely, my dad. I wondered if it had been like that for him, but I knew it hadn't. It *couldn't* have felt like being underwater. Because my dad, I was pretty sure, had died in the heat of fire.

One day, at lunch, I was sitting all by myself, as usual, in the refectory and Tyro—who also happened to be alone, without his usual entourage—

came and sat next to me. I could feel my whole body tense, and I leaned forward as if I needed to protect my food. We were having some kind of dog-foodlike stew, supposedly beef.

Watching me hunched over my stew must have reminded Tyro of the old days, because he said, "Remember when I put all that ketchup on your burger?"

"Yeah," I said warily. "What about it?"

"That was pretty funny, wasn't it?" he said.

"Actually," I said, "it wasn't funny at all. It was really dumb." Strangely, I wasn't scared of him anymore. We'd crossed some border or passed some threshold. We could have been two different people. We were nothing like the bully and the bully-ee we'd been all through the first semester.

"I guess it wasn't that funny," he said. "I'm sorry about that, okay?"

We concentrated on our stew for a while. Then he said, "How's the hospital thing going?"

"It's okay," I said. "There's this one little kid I like. We get along. So it makes it sort of fun." I stopped myself, not wanting to tell him any more about Nola. It was as if telling him might spoil everything, as if he might decide to take it all away from me. What if he persuaded his dad to switch our jobs? Then he would get to go to the hospital, and Nola would be his friend instead of mine.

"How's the homeless thing?" I said. "I'll bet that's really . . . rewarding."

"It's all right, I guess. A lot of the guys smell really bad. And last week, one guy pulled a knife on another guy and got kicked out of the shelter. That was exciting, for about two minutes. Otherwise, it's mostly boring. And the food I have to dish out is totally gross and repulsive. It makes this shit look like something you'd get at a fancy restaurant in the city."

"That's hard to imagine," I said.

"Don't try," he said. "You don't want to."

I laughed. It wasn't funny, but it was funny enough.

"How are things going otherwise?" he asked. I wondered why he was asking until I remembered that he was supposed to be my Big Brother.

"Fine," I said. "Everything's fine." And that was that. We ate our lunch, and the lunch period ended, and we went back to our classes as if there had never been any bad feeling between us, as if we were just two guys—the Big Brother and the new student he'd been asked to watch over— meeting for a friendly catch-up session after the official phase of their relationship, the Big Brother–Little Brother part, was officially over.

CHAPTER TWELVE

ONE AFTERNOON, A few weeks before spring break, I went to see Nola and she wasn't in her room.

Not only was her bed empty, but it looked as if she'd moved out. The stuffed animals were gone, and there was nothing there but the empty bed and the yellow walls that Nola claimed that she'd turned yellow to match. My first thought was that Nola was cured and they'd sent her home. I wondered if I would still be allowed to visit her, if we could still be friends. Even though I'd hoped she would recover, somehow I'd never planned for the possibility that she might not be in the hospital forever, and that our friendship wouldn't go on exactly the way it was.

Then another thought occurred to me, and suddenly I was afraid that Nola had died. I was shaking so hard that, before I left the room, I had to go into the bathroom and splash cold water on my face because I thought I was going to throw up.

I ran to Mrs. Straus's office.

"Oh, Bart," she said. "I'm so sorry. I've been trying to reach you all day, but I think I must have the wrong number for you."

I turned my phone on and flipped it open: six missed calls.

"We're not allowed to keep our phones on at school," I said.

"Oh, dear, I wish you had gotten the message," she said. "Because I would have told you not to come."

"Where's Nola?"

"She's had a little setback," said Mrs. Straus. "She's been moved to the pediatric step-down unit."

"What's a step-down unit?" I asked.

"It's a place where the nurses can watch the kids more closely," said Mrs. Straus.

"Why do they need to watch her?"

"She was having some trouble breathing. Nothing serious, nothing that hasn't happened before—"

"What do you mean, *trouble*?"

Mrs. Straus put her arm around my shoulders.

"Bart, honey," she said, "maybe you should just go home this afternoon. I'm not sure they'll let you see her in the unit. In fact, I'm almost positive they won't. I'll keep in touch with you by phone. I promise I'll call. I'll let you know how she's doing. And as soon as this little crisis is over, you can come visit her again."

I didn't like the sound of it. I didn't like it at all.

"When is it going to be over?" I asked.

"What?" said Mrs. Straus.

"Nola's setback," I said.

"That's hard to predict," said Mrs. Straus.

"So how do you know it *will* be over?"

Mrs. Straus sighed. "Because this isn't the first time. It's happened before. And she's always pulled through. Nola's a strong girl."

That made me feel a little better. But not much.

"I want to see her," I said. "I'm not going home till I see her."

"Okay, said Mrs. Straus. "You two are such good buddies, it might make Nola feel better to see you. But I can't promise anything. And if they *do* let you see her, it will only be for a few minutes."

"Fine," I said. "A few minutes will be fine. I just want to say hi."

Mrs. Straus led me down the corridor to another wing of the hospital. And I could tell—just as I could tell about the visitors getting off at the different floors that first day in the elevator—

that things were more serious here, sadder and more dangerous. No one looked at anyone else, no one smiled, and the waiting room was filled with family members talking quietly on their cell phones, or holding on to one another, or dozing on the chairs, under blankets, as if they'd been there for days. As if they'd left their homes and moved into the waiting room and were camped out, waiting for some signal that would allow them to go see a desperately sick relative.

Mrs. Straus flashed her ID badge at a sensor on the wall, and a door swung open. I could feel the eyes of the waiting-room families drilling into the back of my head. Who were *we* to be getting this special privilege? No one, I wanted to tell them. Just a kid who trashed another kid's SUV and was getting punished, I realized now, in a way that was much more painful than anything Tyro's dad or the school could have dreamed up to make me pay.

Nola's bed was in a room with four other beds. In the bed nearest the window lay a kid who kept yelling and groaning, Nola was hooked up to more tubes than she had been before. She had an oxygen mask over her face, and up above her bed were all sorts of monitors with charts and readouts and digital numbers that kept rising and falling. My first thought was that this was all a big mistake, that Nola didn't belong here, that she was supposed to be back in her room with the goofy stuffed animals and get-well cards.

Her eyes were closed. She was sleeping, breathing through the oxygen mask. I didn't want to wake her, I didn't want to see her here, and I didn't think she wanted me to see her like this. She looked sicker, frailer, even more yellow—

Suddenly Mrs. Straus piped up in her supercheery voice, "Nola! Look who's here to see you!"

Nola opened her eyes, and she was Nola again. She raised one eyebrow and motioned for me to come closer. She slipped the oxygen mask off her mouth and whispered in my ear, "Get me out of here! Now!"

"I'm working on it," I said.

And I was. My brain was going a mile a minute, trying to come up with some new escape plan: Let's see. We might have to bop that nurse over the head, and steal her uniform, and . . . But that wouldn't work.

"Excuse me, young man, but are you a member of the immediate family?" It was a nurse.

I'm her brother, I wanted to say. I knew that would have been okay with Nola. But it would have felt weird, lying in front of Mrs. Straus, so I just shook my head no.

"I'm sorry," said the nurse, "but only immediate family are allowed in the unit, and only for the first ten minutes after the hour."

"We understand," said Mrs. Straus. "Bart's a friend. He just wanted a word with Nola. We're leaving right away."

"See you tomorrow," I told Nola, though I suddenly remembered that the next day was Saturday. Even if I could sneak into the unit, how would I get to the hospital?

"See you tomorrow," Nola said. "Don't forget, okay?" And she winked.

That night, at dinner, I started telling Mom about what had happened with Nola that day, and I started crying. It was really embarrassing. Because ever since September, I'd been trying not to break down around Mom, no matter what.

People were doing enough crying in those days, and I felt that seeing me cry would only make things worse for Mom. But I couldn't help it, I kept seeing Nola in that room, with the kid yelling and moaning and the two other kids I couldn't even look at. I kept seeing her raise her eyebrow, and I recalled her asking me to get her out of there, even though we both knew that I couldn't get her out, I couldn't do anything, there was no way I could help her. Then I would remember her telling me not to forget about coming to see her tomorrow.

"I want to see her," I told Mom.

"We can go tomorrow," said Mom. "I'll drive

you to the hospital."

"You don't need to come upstairs if you don't want to," I said. It seemed like the wrong moment to introduce Mom to Nola. Mom would never know what Nola had really been like. The picture she'd have in her mind was Nola tied up to the tubes and monitors and hardly able to talk. And that wasn't Nola at all.

"Fine," Mom said. "I'm sure there's a cafeteria. I'll get a cup of coffee and wait for you. I don't think they'll let you stay very long, anyway."

"You're the greatest," I told her.

"No," said Mom. "*You* are. And I want you to know I'm really proud of you. I'm proud I raised a person like you."

I wanted to thank her, to tell her it was because she was the way *she* was, but now it was all *much* too embarrassing, and I mumbled something and left the table.

"Put your dish in the sink," said Mom, and somehow I knew that she knew what I wanted to say, and couldn't.

That night, I couldn't sleep. I kept having crazy dreams. You'd think I would have had hospital nightmares, after the day I'd had. But my dreams were full of bright colors and exotic animals and tropical sunsets. I woke in the middle of the night and thought: I'm dreaming Nola's dreams. It should have made me feel better, as if we were still in communication. But it only made me feel more frightened and alone.

CHAPTER THIRTEEN

THE NEXT DAY, SATURDAY, Mom drove me to the hospital, just as she'd promised. I was worried that she'd forget she'd offered to wait in the cafeteria, and that she might insist on coming with me. I knew she'd want to be with me in case I had to deal with something difficult or painful. But she headed off to the cafeteria, saying, "Take as long as you want. As long as they let you. But don't get in anyone's way. I'll be here whenever you get back. Don't worry, I've got a book."

For a moment I was afraid that I wouldn't be

able to find the room where they'd taken Nola, because I'd been so upset yesterday, and Mrs. Straus had led me—well, practically dragged me—to the right place. But in fact I found my way straight there, or at least to the waiting room, where, because it was the weekend, there were even more families than the day before. I hovered around by the locked door until a nurse went in, and I followed her. What did I have to lose? If they caught me, all they could do was kick me out.

After a few moments of trying to look like I knew where I was going, I found Nola's room. The kid by the window was still crying out in pain. I recognized the other two kids.

But now there was someone else in Nola's bed.

"Where is she?" I asked the nurse.

"Who?" the nurse said.

"Nola," I said, and at that moment I realized that, after all this time, I didn't even know her last name. How would I find her? I felt as if I had lost her and I would never see her again.

"Oh, right," said the nurse. "I remember you. You're the kid who was here yesterday when you weren't supposed to be. The friend."

"That's me," I said. "The friend."

"She's been moved to the ICU," said the nurse.

"What's that?" I said, though I sort of knew.

"The intensive care unit."

"What do you mean? Has she gotten worse? Is she okay?"

The nurse just stared at me, sympathetic and impatient at the same time. She had work to do. What part of "intensive care unit" was I not understanding?

"Is she going to get better?" I asked.

She said, "We hope so."

"Where's the ICU?" I asked.

"Up on the fifteenth floor. But they're not going to let you in. For one thing—"

"Thanks," I said, not wanting to waste the time it would take her to tell me why I wasn't going to be allowed to see Nola.

The elevator was taking forever to come. I gave up and ran up the stairs, so I was sweaty and panting by the time I got to the fifteenth floor. I found the locked door, and I waited till a guy in a white coat went in, and I sneaked in behind him. I was getting good at this, though it was a skill I hoped never to have to use again.

Once more I tried to look as if I knew what I was doing and where I was going, as if I was a close family member. I peeked into every cubicle I passed, but I couldn't see Nola. Most of the patients were ancient, and every one of them seemed to be in bad shape.

Finally, just as I turned a corner at the end of the hall, I saw something so shocking that I stopped dead because I simply could not understand, could not compute, what I was seeing. Gathered around one of the beds was a group of people I recognized. I knew them from somewhere, but it took me a really long time to figure out who they were.

It was Tyro and his family, his mother and

father, and a girl, a little younger than Tyro. They stood around a bed, looking down, and though my first impulse was to back away, I was still so confused that I went closer.

In the bed was Nola. Her eyes were shut, her chin was nearly touching her chest. She was breathing very rapidly and shallowly. And I knew, without anyone having to tell me, that she was dying.

But there were a lot of other things that I didn't know. Mysteries and riddles. All sorts of questions ran through my mind, and I wondered if I would ever find out the answers. Had the Bergens known that I was visiting Nola? Did Tyro know? Had Nola been aware that I was the person who'd scratched up her brother's Escalade? And all this time I'd imagined that I was the only one with secrets. . . .

Just at that moment, the family spotted me. They looked surprised but not half so surprised as I was. I saw Tyro clench his fists and then unclench them as he looked at me. Then Tyro's mom reached out and drew me in and pulled me to her side, and everyone began weeping softly.

"We're so grateful, Bart," Tyro's mom said. "Nola told us all about your friendship."

But Nola hadn't told me about *them*. She must have known the whole story, not at first, but maybe after she mentioned to her family she had a new friend, a visitor on some punishment detail for having done something bad at his school, and they'd put two and two together. It all added up, because maybe the experience of having a daughter in the hospital had made Tyro's dad think of the Reach Out program in the first place. But why hadn't anyone let me in on the truth?

Maybe Nola wanted it kept secret. Maybe she was afraid that if I knew she was Tyro's sister, after what he'd done to me—and maybe she knew what he was like, how mean he could be—I wouldn't want to be her friend or visit her anymore.

"You helped her so much," Tyro's dad said. "You—" He couldn't go on. Tears were streaming down his cheeks. I didn't ever want to see someone like Tyro's dad cry!

"You did so much to make her last days happier," Mrs. Bergen added. Her last days! Was this another little detail that everyone but me had known all along? Did everybody know that Nola wasn't going to live very long, and I'd been the only one stupid enough to think she might get better and that we might go on being friends, and I could watch her get stronger and grow up?

I felt like they'd been plotting, and that this was a million times worse than Tyro and his gang scheming to torture or even kill me. I couldn't have said *why* it was worse, but I felt in my heart that it was, and I wanted to tell them how dishonest and selfish they'd been.

But of course I couldn't say anything like that to the grieving family of a little girl who wasn't going to live much longer. Anyway, they hadn't planned *all* of it. Who could have predicted that, of all the kids in the hospital, the one I would get close to was Nola? It could just as easily have been Ramón or Stimmer, the first kids I met. But it *couldn't* have been them, it could only have been Nola.

I felt the tears welling up in my eyes, and even under the circumstances—which, anyone would have admitted, were pretty extraordinary—the last thing in the world I wanted was to cry in front of Tyro. Even though Tyro was crying, along with everyone in his family. Even so, I would rather have died myself before I let the king of the Bullywell bullies see me dissolve in hysterics.

"I'm sorry, I'm so sorry" was all I could say. Then I turned and ran, back past the doctors and families, past the sick old people in their curtained alcoves. No one stopped me, no one said a word. A few nurses watched me streak past. I had the feeling that, if they'd worked there awhile, they'd seen everything. They were probably used to people tearing out of the ICU.

On the way down, the elevator stopped at every floor even though it was empty and no one got on. It seemed like another part of the plot. Only now it was a plot to keep me from reaching my mom. Finally I found the main floor and the cafeteria, and there she was, reading her book at a table in the sunlight and looking completely beautiful.

"Bart!" she said. "Sweetheart, what's wrong?" But now I was crying too hard to talk, and at the same time I was strangely aware of the people around us at the other tables, watching me cry.

"Let's get out of here," I told Mom.

"My thinking exactly," Mom said.

She literally tucked me under her arm like a mother duck protecting her duckling, and whisked me out of the cafeteria and the hospital and clear across the parking lot. Neither of us said a word until we were in the car. Then I told her what had happened, how I'd gotten to the ICU and known Nola was dying, and how I'd seen her family and realized that she was Tyro's sister.

I could tell that Mom was stunned. At least *she* wasn't in on the secret. But she didn't say anything for a long time, she just kept driving calmly.

Finally she said, "None of that matters, honey.

Not Nola's parents, not Tyro. I mean, *of course* they matter. But right now, right at this moment, they're not what should matter to *you*. They're not what you should be thinking about. What's important is the friendship you had with Nola, the fact that you two cared about each other, and that you *did* make her life better, at the end when she really needed it."

At this, I started crying again, and Mom was crying, too, but she kept on talking through her tears.

"And you'll never lose that," she said. "It's something you'll have forever. The memory will be like your guardian angel, especially as time passes, and the painful stuff falls away, and you remember all the good things you had with that person."

It struck me that what she was saying had something to do with her and Dad, or with me and Dad. Or with both of us and Dad.

I took a deep breath. Then I said, "Do you miss him?"

"Yes," said Mom. "I always did. Even when I was angry. And now I'm not angry anymore. Just sad."

"Me, too," I said.

Mom said, "You think you'll feel like this forever. But you won't, honey. I promise. Little by little, day by day, you'll feel better. The pain will be a little duller, a tiny bit less sharp. On some days, you'll feel worse again, and you'll think it's as bad as it was at the beginning. But the next day, you'll feel a little more cheerful. And one day you'll actually feel happy again."

"When will that be?"

"In time," Mom said. "Time's got to pass."

"I feel a little better already," I said. And then we both got quiet as I tried to figure out why I'd said that. Because, in a way, it was true. And in another way, it wasn't. It felt good to finally talk about Dad with Mom. But I still missed my father, the pain hadn't dulled at all, and I knew that the sharp pain of missing Nola was only just beginning.

CHAPTER FOURTEEN

TYRO WAS ABSENT from school for a week. Word got around that his sister had died. Everyone said how tragic it was, and it made me feel even worse that there was no one I trusted enough to tell about Nola's having been my friend. I guess I should have been used to it, after all the practice I'd had, not being able to talk to anyone about my dad.

I realized that losing Nola wasn't the same for me as it must have been for Tyro. She was his sister, and I'd only known her for a few months. But somehow that didn't make me any less sad.

I wondered if, when Tyro returned to school, we'd be able to talk about Nola. He would know that I'd known her better than anyone else at school, except him, and that I understood, better than anyone, what he'd lost. We would talk about how awesome she'd been. And maybe it would comfort us both, just a little.

I had the picture—the whole scene, and how it was going to play out—fixed so firmly in my mind that when I walked into school the next Monday morning, and Tyro was the first person I saw, I had trouble putting the real person together with the fantasy I'd been having. He was standing all alone in the center of the main hall. None of his friends were around. I had the feeling that he'd been looking for me, waiting for me. And it made sense, because I'd been hoping to see him, too.

I stood directly in front of him. Neither of us spoke or moved. Until at last I said, "I'm really sorry about Nola."

He looked at me, but he seemed to be seeing

something—or someone—else. Then his face changed and took on an expression I'd never seen on anyone's face before. Part furious, part sad, part distant, part . . . I didn't know what it was.

And then he hauled off and punched me, with all his might, in the stomach.

In the instant before the pain began, it crossed my mind that the story wasn't supposed to end this way. Our shared sorrow and grief were supposed to make us friends, to bring us closer together, to make us more compassionate, just as Dr. Bratwurst was always saying. That's how it would have ended in a book, all neat and tidy, with everyone learning and changing and growing and becoming better people because of what they'd suffered.

But that wasn't how it was turning out. Because this was real life, and messy. The story had its own direction, its own end, and I felt like an actor in someone else's play, letting the director guide me.

I made a fist and pulled my arm back as far as it would go.

I hit Tyro as hard as I could.

In a moment we were all over each other, swinging and pushing and grabbing for each other's throats. I thought we were going to kill each other. I knew that was what we both wanted. He kept hitting me, harder and harder, but the strangest thing was, it still didn't hurt, because I was so focused on smashing him.

Each time I hit him, it was like there was something behind it, aiming my fist, a force that was making me pound him harder and land my punches where they might do the most damage. I hit him once for Nola, and for how unfair it was that she'd died. One punch for every time he'd made me miserable since I came to Bullywell, one for the ketchup, one each for the names, the kicks, the locker, the text message supposedly from my dad. And then I was hitting him for my dad. One punch for Dad leaving us for Caroline, two more for the towers and the planes flying into them, more punches for my dad getting killed when so many others were saved, another for my mom's close call.

All the time I was hitting him I didn't think about how, after all this time, I was finally standing up for myself, fighting back against the bully. Against all the bullies, everywhere. Because Bullyville *was* everywhere, it wasn't just this school. Everybody was being bullied by someone or something—by mean kids or terrorists, by the total unfairness of bad luck and sadness and death. Me, Mom and Dad, Nola, poor old Bern, even Tyro—we were all being pushed around by something we couldn't help and couldn't control.

As I slammed my fist into Tyro, I didn't think about whether this was the right or the wrong way to deal with it, or if I was right or wrong. I didn't think how awful it was to hit a guy whose little sister had just died. I didn't think that he'd hit me first, that he'd slugged a kid whose dad had been killed on 9/11. All I thought about was punching him, and it wasn't even really like thinking. It was just something my body was doing, independent of my brain and disconnected from the part of myself that I thought of as *me*.

Even as I was slugging away at Tyro, memories were coming back to me, all sorts of things I'd forgotten, that I hadn't *let* myself remember. Things I hadn't *wanted* to remember. But now it all rushed in, all the times my dad and I had had fun, the circus and the zoo, the sweltering day he'd rescued me and taken me home, defying the Little League coach who'd ordered our team to run twenty laps as punishment for losing a game. I heard him cheering for me at those games, and I heard him laugh when my stupid cousin painted my fingernails at Gran's Thanksgiving. I kept hearing him laugh, along with Mom, at all their little private jokes. They were always laughing. And when I'd ask what they were laughing at, they would always explain, so I never felt left out.

I hit Tyro again for how my dad died without my getting a chance to talk to him and ask him what he thought he was doing when he moved out. Or whether he really loved me, like he said on the messages he left, and whether he was planning to come back home and live with us again.

Meanwhile, Tyro and I kept at it, slugging each other. Tyro's face was all bloody, so mine probably was, too.

Finally, after a very long time, I felt someone yanking back on my arms and shoulders. A crowd had formed, and someone was dragging us apart. I saw Dr. Bratwurst, and the teachers, and the other kids. Blood was running into my eyes.

And then it was over.

I never went back to Bullywell. That was my last day. There was one final meeting, this time with just Mom and me and Dr. Bratwurst, who calmly explained that Bullywell and I just weren't a perfect fit. Not the match that everyone had hoped for.

I didn't bother mentioning that Tyro had hit me first. I didn't care about justice. I was glad I was leaving. The school had taught me everything that it was ever going to teach me. I thought: Just let me out of Bullywell and everything will work out.

And things *did* work out. Luckily for me, my former babysitter, Ivy, had taken the second semester off from college because she'd broken up with her boyfriend and failed biology and was thinking she didn't want to go to medical school after all. Mom hired her to babysit me — although we called it homeschooling — until the school year was out.

Ivy wasn't in the greatest shape herself, but she was a good driver, and she liked to go places. Sometimes we'd take the train into Manhattan and look at museums, or go to the park and sit there. We went to the Bronx Zoo and rode the Staten Island Ferry. Every so often we'd read a book, or she'd teach me something she remembered from high school science or math, so we could feel honest about the homeschooling part.

The next fall, Ivy returned to college and I went back to public school. And within a few days, all my old friends were my friends again. It was almost as if I'd never left. Sometimes someone would ask me how my time at Bullywell had been, and I'd say: Worse than you could imagine.

A year later, my mom met a really nice guy named Rob, and the year after that, they got married. Their wedding was covered by several newspapers, because at that point the papers were running feel-good stories about people managing to glue their lives back together after everything got blown apart for them on September 11. Miracle Boy and his mom and the new stepdad— it made really great copy.

A lot of the stories talked about us mending and healing and moving on. But of course nothing broken is ever completely fixed. There's always that hairline crack you can see if you look hard enough.

I tried to tell that part to the reporters. But somehow that never made it into the papers.

After enough time had passed, everything that happened that year did start to seem like the crack you can see in a piece of china that's been shattered and repaired, or an arm or leg that's been broken and mended but is never quite straight.

Close enough, everyone says. And it was, it was close enough. Though *close enough*, as everyone knows, doesn't mean: *the way it was before*.

Years later, after I grew up and had a family of my own, we'd come back to visit my mom and Rob. The first time my two kids were old enough to understand, I pointed up the mountain and Baileywell Castle, looming above the town.

I said, "I used to go there for a while."

"Creepy," my older son said. And that was it. I was glad that, for some reason, they never asked how it was. I could never bring myself to talk about my year at Bullywell.

I would have, if my kids had been bullied at their schools. I would have told them the same thing happened to me. I would have said, Look at me, I survived. I would have told them, if they needed me to. But I was glad they didn't.

No one bullied my kids, and I know they didn't

259

see their dad as a former bully-ee. *I* knew I was the same person: an older, bigger Bart. But I no longer felt like that bullied kid, the kid who went to Bullywell, that year I was in the wrong place at definitely the wrong time.